FYODOR MIKHAILOVICH DOSTOEVSKY's life was as dark and dramatic as the great novels he wrote. He was born in Moscow in 1821, the son of a former army surgeon whose drunken brutality led his own serfs to murder him by pouring vodka down his throat until he strangled. A short first novel, *Poor Folk* (1846), brought him instant success, but his writing career was cut short by his arrest for alleged subversion against Tsar Nicholas I in 1849. In prison he was given the "silent treatment" for eight months (guards even wore velvet-soled boots) before he was led in front of a firing squad. Dressed in a death shroud, he faced an open grave and awaited his execution when, suddenly, an order arrived commuting his sentence. He then spent four years at hard labor in a Siberian prison, where he began to suffer from epilepsy, and he only returned to St. Petersburg a full ten years after he had left in chains.

His prison experiences coupled with his conversion to a conservative and profoundly religious philosophy formed the basis for his great novels. But it was his fortuitous marriage to Anna Snitkina, following a period of utter destitution brought about by his compulsive gambling, that gave Dostoevsky the emotional stability to complete *Crime and Punishment* (1866), *The Idiot* (1868–69), *The Possessed* (1871–72), and *The Brothers Karamazov* (1879–80). When Dostoevsky died in 1881, hc left a legacy of masterworks that influenced the great thinkers and writers of the Western world and immortalized him as a giant among writers of world literature.

NOTES FROM UNDERGROUND

FYODOR DOSTOEVSKY

Translated by Mirra Ginsburg

With an Introduction by Donald Fanger

BANTAM CLASSIC

NOTES FROM UNDERGROUND
A Bantam Book

PUBLISHING HISTORY
Notes from Underground was first published in 1864
First Bantam edition published December 1974
Bantam Classics edition published October 1981
Bantam reissue published March 1992
Bantam mass market edition / April 2005

Published by
Bantam Dell
A Division of Random House, Inc.
New York, New York

Bantam Books and the rooster colophon are registered trademarks of
Random House, Inc.

ISBN 0-553-21144-7

Printed in the United States of America
Published simultaneously in Canada

www.bantamdell.com

OPM   37 36 35 34 33 32 31 29 28

CONTENTS

INTRODUCTION

IN THE 110 years since its first publication, *Notes from Underground* has lost none of its power to fascinate—to provoke, worry, repel, baffle, and move. If anything, that power has grown with time. The paradoxes of the nameless narrator resonate for us as they could not have done for Dostoevsky's contemporaries, for the political cataclysms and cultural revolutions of our century compel us to recognize (if not embrace) the kinship on which he insists, to see something of ourselves in his caricature. Freud and the whole body of specifically "modern" literature—including Dostoevsky's own later novels—have furnished a set of contexts that make his terms intelligible, even familiar. They also confirm the status of *Notes from Underground* as one of the most sheerly astonishing and subversive creations of European fiction.

This is not simply a matter of "content," of the character's "painful and scornful conclusions," or even (the words are Thomas Mann's) of his corrosive "radical frankness." More important is the way Dostoevsky alters the rules of the literary game—and forces us to learn them as we go. "A novel requires a hero," his wily soliloquist acknowledges, "but here there's a *deliberate* collection of all the traits for an antihero.... All this will produce an extremely unpleasant impression." "And yet," he taunts his reader, "I may even be more 'alive' than you are. Do take a closer look!"

There is no avoiding the invitation. This "confession" (as Dostoevsky first entitled it) begins with "I," but it ends provocatively with "we"; in fact, the speaker has involved the reader from the beginning, addressing him directly, anticipating his reactions, preempting his judgments, denying him the comfortable role of spectator. (Just so Baudelaire challenges the reader of his *Fleurs du mal:* "Hypocrite *lecteur!—mon semblable, mon frère*..." The underground man, in short, traps his reader into a relationship.

It is worth insisting on this fact because it can guard us against tempting simplifications. The *Notes* abound in propositions about questions that continue to concern our age: self-knowledge and self-definition, the loneliness of urban man, the nature (and value!) of happiness, the power of ideology, the intrications of spirit, and the obduracy of flesh. That is why Dostoevsky's text has proven so legitimately attractive to students of philosophy, psychology, intellectual and political history. But these propositions must not be taken as expressing Dostoevsky's views—or even, simply, those of his character.

Already with his first novel, *Poor People,* Dostoevsky complained about the way readers tended to confuse him with his hero. "They are used to seeing the writer's mug in everything," he wrote his brother, "but I haven't shown mine. It never occurred to them that it's Devushkin [his character] speaking, not I, and that Devushkin cannot speak in any other way." The point is crucial: Dostoevsky, a relatively undistinguished thinker outside his fiction, was a genius at dramatizing ideas, bringing them to incandescent life, setting them in confrontation with each other, and testing them in action. All his novels are a play, however serious, with ideas. The *responsibility* for any given view belongs to the character enunciating it, and—just as in life—we must take into account all that we know and suspect of that character if we are to understand what he says.

In *Notes from Underground,* for example, the underground man's monologue moves strikingly from what is most personal to what is most general. His views arise from experience, his experience corroborates the views;

each seems to authenticate the other. But which are we to take as primary? The question is important—and unanswerable. Is he really proving that modern urban man can neither do nor become anything? Or is he constructing a casuistical theory to excuse his own failures? We choose either answer at our peril because, after all, *he* has given us the choice. There is no other, because there is no other material than what he presents. Yet if we accept it as offered, we have entered his own endless dilemma.

Here is a central feature of that special *kind* of fiction Dostoevsky created in the great novels beginning with *Crime and Punishment*: the tendency to parcel out to his characters portions of his own beliefs and doubts, mixing truths and half-truths, qualifying a statement through the tone of voice in which it is uttered, having the utterer himself call it into question elsewhere—and all in the absence of any such authoritative author's voice as might provide some ultimate point of view in more conventional novels.

Notes from Underground, published in 1864, is Dostoevsky's first essay in this new kind of fiction, and it broaches a new set of concerns. It shows him on the threshold of his major period, discovering the enabling device that would produce, over the next decade and a half, *Crime and Punishment, The Idiot, The Possessed, A Raw Youth,* and *The Brothers Karamazov.* But it does more than open the way to these great works; for it grows directly out of his earlier writings and constitutes an implicit critique of them. Few careers show such clear turning points. So it may be well to approach the *Notes* by way of their Dostoevskian ancestry.

I. BEGINNINGS: 1846–1863

Dostoevsky (1821–1881) was nineteenth-century Russia's only great novelist of the city—in his own words, the poet of the "accidental tribe," by which he meant all those who were rootless, divorced from tradition and traditional assurance. His first novel was *Poor People*; his second, *The Double*, was subtitled "A Petersburg Poem." Virtually all his work through *Notes from Underground* fits under these rubrics, dealing (to invoke yet another of his titles) with "the insulted and injured." He was to pursue the theme of alienation throughout his career, but he saw it at first largely in the forms of poverty and failure.

Dostoevsky's city was Petersburg (now Leningrad)— "the most abstract and intentional city on earth," as the underground man calls it. Unlike the other capitals of Europe, Petersburg had no long history as a settled place. The site, indeed, seemed almost uninhabitable—a low-lying swamp on the Gulf of Finland—when Peter the Great brought it into being by imperial fiat at the beginning of the eighteenth century and made it the seat of government. The tsar himself laid out the symmetrical streets; Italian and French architects produced magnificent palaces; and the place was populated by edict. Petersburg was literally born of an idea, against nature, more sheerly man-made than any comparable city in Europe. By Dostoevsky's time, it was beginning to share the problems of the modern metropolis in general, but its almost metaphysical distinctiveness could never be forgotten. Thus it enjoyed a double existence, as fact and as symbol, the fantastic locus of a life removed from nature, community, and historical continuity.

Poor People was published in January 1846, and was immediately recognized as a major event in Russian literature. Dostoevsky later recalled how, as a twenty-four-year-old novice, he had been summoned to meet Belinsky, the most influential critic of his time: " 'But do you, you yourself, understand,' he repeated to me several times, screaming as was his habit, 'what you have written?!' He always screamed when he spoke in a state of great agitation. 'You may have written, guided by instinct, as an artist, but have you yourself grasped this dreadful truth which you have pointed out to us? It is impossible that at the age of twenty [*sic*] you could have understood it.' "

The "dreadful truth" concerned the hopeless lives of the Petersburg poor; Dostoevsky had produced Russia's first social novel. And he had done it by an astonishing act of creative empathy—not by commenting as narrator, but by doing without a narrator altogether. *Poor People* is a novel in letters; two fully individual human voices body forth the drama. The man in question, Makar Devushkin, is an aging civil servant, one of that hitherto faceless crowd of copying clerks which constituted a large part of the city's population in Dostoevsky's time. Earlier writers had treated them more or less ironically as a class or a problem. Now Dostoevsky approached them as self-conscious subjects. He even has Devushkin read the greatest of earlier stories about his own type (Gogol's "The Overcoat"), only to reject it indignantly, partly for its wounding accuracy but also for its larger inaccuracy in denying the poor clerk's humanity, his doomed quest for recognition and dignity. "I have no polish or style," Devushkin himself admits; "all the same, I am a man, in heart and mind a man!" "The poor man looks at God's world differently," he proclaims elsewhere, and the book exists to explain how.

Already in his first work, then, Dostoevsky is concerned with creating an inner world of experience, which refracts the outer world but is not determined by it—and is expressed by a character whose style may vie in importance with what he says. Here, as in his last novel, *The Brothers Karamazov*, Dostoevsky uses literature to create literature. His people are readers and writers whose demonstrated tastes and skills not only help us understand them but constitute an oblique polemic with other Russian writers. Already, too, he invests the humblest detail with explosive psychological significance: Devushkin sees a loose button as robbing him of the last shreds of his dignity in a tense interview, just as the underground man will later suffer agonies over a yellow spot on his trousers. Anything—the more ludicrous the better—can trigger pathos in Dostoevsky's world (compare the underground man's reference to "these dirtiest, most ludicrous, most terrible minutes of my entire life"). And scenes of scandal are forever threatening—to confirm and fuel the latent desperation of these characters.

The Double, Dostoevsky's second novel, appeared two weeks after *Poor People.* "It will be my masterpiece," he confided to his brother; it was "ten times better" than his first work. Few readers agreed, and the author himself later admitted that the tale was flawed. But he maintained to the end of his life that the idea had been a felicitous one, and he declared that he had never broached a more serious one in all his writing. That idea, in the words of one Russian critic, centers on the "ontological instability of personality."

The story, steeped in grotesquerie, traces the slip into madness of yet another poor Petersburg copying clerk. Like *Poor People,* it is a polemical reworking of motifs from the stories of Nikolai Gogol, Dostoevsky's great predecessor in Russian fiction. Yakov Petrovich Golyadkin, the central character, is a pitiful nonentity—like Poprishchin, the protagonist of Gogol's "Diary of a Madman." Increasingly he seeks escape from an intolerable existence by nourishing dreams of grandeur, which soon take form in the imaginary person of his double, "Mr. Golyadkin, Junior." There is none of the Gogolian pathos at the end of this story, and Dostoevsky shows little overt sympathy with his hero, whose ideals as represented by his double turn out to be shabby, a desire for "success" at the office and romance with the boss's daughter. It is a shrewd and tough-minded view that Dostoevsky takes of his character. But already, here, we meet what was to become another characteristic tendency of his writing: the creation of bizarre and distasteful characters whose common humanity we are forced to perceive in spite of our repugnance.

Golyadkin is the first in a long line of split personalities in Dostoevsky's work—but split in a special way, not between "good" and "bad," but between more and less authentic. *The Double* is rudimentary in this respect by comparison with Dostoevsky's mature works, for the latter show characters attempting to live out ideas, finding what is authentic in themselves by experience pro and contra. (So in *Crime and Punishment* Raskolnikov kills the old pawnbroker to prove that he is an "exceptional man," a Napoleon who need not be bound by the moral scruples of the herd; but his subsequent experience—his punishment— shows him unable to sustain this role, burdened with a sense of transgression which his reason had not foreseen.) In *The Double* we have simply pathological bravado. "You all know me, gentlemen," Mr. Golyadkin declares at one point, "but up to now you have only known one side of me." The other side, he hints (anticipating the underground man), is above worldly concerns—magnanimous, perhaps even heroic. "There are people," he remarks, "who don't say they're happy and enjoying life to the full just because their trousers fit well, for instance." His boldest resolutions expire comically. Shall he enter his chief's party (to which he has not been invited)? He ponders on the landing: "Shall I? . . . Yes, I will—why shouldn't I? The brave go where they please." "Thus reassuring himself," Dostoevsky comments, "our hero suddenly and quite unexpectedly withdrew behind the screen." (Compare the underground man at the excruciating dinner in the Hôtel de Paris: "Now's just the right moment to throw a bottle at them all, I thought, and, picking up a bottle, I . . . poured myself a full glass.") Dostoevsky's ironic comment about Golyadkin—that "he was neither dead nor alive, but somewhere in between"—applies with even greater force to the underground man. Both are quintessential denizens—symbolic emanations—of the spectral capital of all the Russias.

In his journalism of 1847 and in the stories of 1847–1848 ("The Landlady," "A Faint Heart," "White Nights"), Dostoevsky anatomizes a new Petersburg type. Hemmed in by a city in which Nature has no place, frustrated by the empty routines of the metropolis, thirsting for direct, spontaneous life, "a man becomes at length not a man but some strange creature of an intermediate sort—a *dreamer*." Such an individual, he says, "is always difficult because he is uneven to an extreme," "tending to settle for the most part in profound isolation, in inaccessible corners, as if hiding from people and from the light." There is a larger share of autobiography in the characterization of this type than in anything Dostoevsky had written previously. The dreamer is an educated man; if he talks like a book (as the underground man will do with Liza), it is because his dreams are literary. In books he finds a life incomparably richer, fuller, more colorful and harmonious than what actually exists around him, and into this fantasy world he rapturously withdraws, out of time and away from the world of contingency. Isolated like Dostoevsky's other early characters in the anonymity of the city, the dreamer differs from them in enjoying a *willed* isolation. The dreamer-narrator of "White Nights" knows that a time may come when he would be glad to trade all his years of fantasy for one day of real life—"but so far that threatening time has not arrived," and he desires nothing "because he is above desire, because he has everything, because he is satiated, because he is the artist of his own life."

Even when he was most alive to the seductions of such a state, however, Dostoevsky could see its destructive side. It was ultimately, he concluded, "a sin and a horror," "a caricature," "a Petersburg nightmare." The "Author's

Note" at the beginning of *Notes from Underground* identifies the underground man precisely as a dreamer of the forties, revisited twenty years after. He can still recall his youthful dreams with emotion—though not without irony. His curse is now that he understands too much, too helplessly.

In the spring of 1849, Dostoevsky was arrested, tried, and sentenced to Siberian prison and exile for his association with the subversive Petrashevsky circle. The real extent of his involvement in revolutionary thought is unclear. So, for that matter, is much of the doctrine he is supposed to have shared—a pre-Marxian, non-"scientific" form of socialism commonly designated as "utopian." Fundamentally religious in nature, it envisaged a future regeneration of the world based on the moral teachings of Christianity. Divine revelation was left moot; the ideal society would in any case be holy. Socialism and Christianity would be merged in a perfect union, a new "religion of humanity." Such a program could accommodate Christian belief intact, but it required an exceedingly optimistic view of human nature. During his eight years in Siberia, Dostoevsky held fast to Christianity, even as he assimilated startlingly new evidence about the nature of man.

That experience, thinly disguised as fiction, is detailed in *Notes from the House of the Dead,* published two years after his return to Petersburg, in 1861. Exposure to types and classes of which he had scarcely been aware before—murderers and thieves, soldiers and peasants—shattered the writer's earlier notions. "Man," he concluded, "is a creature that can get accustomed to anything, and I think that is the best definition of him." A witness to sadism in others, he came to discover its complement in himself, "that malignant pleasure which at times is almost a craving to tear open one's wound on purpose, as though one desired to revel in one's pain, as though the consciousness of one's misery was an actual enjoyment." Here is one of the central themes of the "underground." Such knowledge, of course, complicates any ready sympathy with victims of injustice and precludes any assumption that improving social conditions will automatically liberate the disadvantaged into positive and happy selfhood. Here, too, through personal suffering, Dostoevsky came to another of the major themes of his later fiction: freedom. The underground man's perverse insistence on whim and spite as exercises in personal freedom, more valuable as such than any rationally planned well-being, arises directly from Dostoevsky's psychological observations in prison. In the bizarre outbursts of hitherto docile convicts he saw "simply the poignant, hysterical craving for self-expression, the unconscious yearning for oneself, the desire to assert...one's crushed personality, a desire which suddenly takes hold of one and reaches the pitch of fury, of spite, of mental aberration, of fits and nervous convulsions. So perhaps a man buried alive and awakening in his coffin might beat upon its lid and struggle to fling it off, though of course reason might convince him that all his efforts would be useless; *but the trouble is that it is not a question of reason...*"

The writer's lifelong desire "to find the human in a human being" begins here to work at a new depth, where social position and conventional notions of character threaten to become irrelevant. Man's impulses are contradictory, his behavior unpredictable. In *The Insulted and Injured,* which was published concurrently with *Notes from the House of the Dead,* Dostoevsky gently parodies his own preexile work, leading the good, the kind, the enthusiastic characters to inevitable defeat at the hands of a villain who—for the first time in his work—articulates and embodies a philosophical *idea.*

The later, better-known Dostoevsky is, above all, the

tragedian of ideas. His rootless characters are particularly vulnerable to them: they become possessed, to the point where an idea determines and distorts the consciousness and life of its bearer. This is most evident in *Notes from Underground,* which represents Dostoevsky's sudden mastery of what he called "the idea incarnate," the central feature of the novels that follow. Apart from the incarnation and the drama, which is to say apart from the artistry, Dostoevsky's ideas are interesting chiefly as so much raw material awaiting inspiration. Still, because the terms of his fiction do arise from his deepest concerns, a word about those concerns in the early 1860s may complete this contextual sketch.

In 1863 Dostoevsky published *Winter Notes on Summer Impressions,* a journalistic account of his first trip to Western Europe, undertaken the year before. "I did not see anything properly," he confesses on the opening page, "and what I did see I had no time to examine." This is no travelogue. Preoccupied now with the question of Russia's destiny, already certain that Europe could furnish only negative examples, he sought and found the latter exclusively. Western individualism was repulsive because materialistic; the Crystal Palace and International Exposition of London terrified him, seeming to herald the advent of a purely materialistic utopia: " 'Isn't this the achievement of perfection?' you think. 'Isn't this the ultimate?' . . . Must you not accept this as the final truth and forever hold your peace?' " As for the promise of Western socialism, that is seen in kindred terms. Here the image of the anthill appears, where "everything runs so smoothly, everything is so well regulated, everyone is well fed and happy, and each one knows his task"—and all in return for "just one little drop" of each individual's liberty. Egotistical freedom and mechanistic collectives are both dead ends (as they will be in *Notes from Underground*): the qualifying adjectives do violence to man's spiritual essence. (Thus the writer's scorn for the "scientific" utopia of the radical populist Chernyshevsky, with his belief that reason can rule man and society can be perfected through each man's pursuit of his enlightened self-interest.) *Real* individualism, Dostoevsky suggests in *Winter Notes,* involves self-transcendence, and offers the only free path to fraternal community. It is the way of Christ, "voluntary, fully conscious self-sacrifice... for the benefit of all."

With such questions uppermost in his mind and such a body of work behind him, Dostoevsky set about the masterpiece one could call liminal, in which he brings to the threshold of narrative consciousness "things [every man] is afraid to reveal even to himself" (*Notes,* I, xi). Viewed historically, this short novel stands as well at the threshold of the larger fictions which made Dostoevsky a world figure—and, through them, at the threshold of that modern literary art which still commands our serious, often uncomfortable attention.

II. NOTES FROM UNDERGROUND

Notes from Underground has attracted many labels. Some have seen it as its author's defense of individualism, others as a case history of neurosis, a work of high comedy, or a specimen of modern tragedy. Dostoevsky's text makes each of these interpretations plausible, but finally escapes them all. The best approach may be to put aside the question of what it means in order to consider what it is and how it conveys meaning.

These "notes" are a performance, part tirade, part memoir, by a nameless personage who claims to be writing for himself alone but who consistently manipulates the reader—of whom he is morbidly aware—to the point where there seems to be no judgment the reader can make which the writer has not already made himself. In the absence of any other source of information or perspective, we suffer his contradictions no less helplessly than he does. For Dostoevsky's presence as author is enigmatic and minimal, confined to a paragraph of introduction and three laconic sentences of conclusion.

What can we learn from this framing presence? At the outset, Dostoevsky takes pains to distance himself from his creation, stressing the fictional nature of the latter. "Nevertheless," he adds, "such persons ... not only exist in our society, but indeed must exist, considering the circumstances under which our society has generally been formed." The underground man, then, is to be seen as representative, his "underground" itself a state shared by others and not simply the product of individual pathology or biographical accident. And his representativeness is historical: He is "one of the characters of our recent past," part of "a generation that is still living out its days among us." Internal evidence makes it clear that his generation is that of the 1840s; he shows the fate of the isolated petty clerk and Dostoevskian dreamer twenty years after, surveying his wasted life in the new spiritual climate of the 1860s and at the same time finding some justification for his own grotesque being in the simplistic views of human nature now current. In Part One, "Underground," Dostoevsky notes, "this personage describes himself and his views, and attempts, as it were, to clarify the reasons why he appeared and was bound to appear in our midst." The phrasing is significant. Mentioning the narrator's self and views in one breath raises the question of how they are related—whether we are to understand the views as the product of his wasted life (and so discount them), or whether the views are to be judged independently (lending that life a dignity which experience has denied it). The qualification ("attempts, as it were") only heightens the uncertainty. With that Dostoevsky relinquishes the stage to his character until he reappears to ring down the curtain, ending what his narrator could not bring himself to end, and thereby underlining that sense of perpetual motion which has come to characterize the monologue of this character—whom he now refers to as a "paradoxalist." The two main senses of paradox make this word a key one.

In the first place, paradox suggests something that flies in the face of received opinion, of common sense. The underground man's views abound in this kind of paradox. He dismisses "the laws of nature," and willfully denies that twice two must equal four. But his most disturbing proposition is less eccentric. It may challenge common sense even today—but it underlies most of the art we think of as "modern":

> And why are you so firmly, so solemnly convinced that only the normal and the positive—in short, only well-being—is to man's advantage? . . . After all, man may be fond not only of well-being. Perhaps he is just as fond of suffering? Perhaps suffering is just as much in his interest as well-being? And man is sometimes extremely fond of suffering, to the point of passion, in fact. And here there is no need to consult world history; ask your own self, if you're a man and have lived at all. As for my personal opinion, it's even somehow indecent to love only well-being. (I, ix)

This must not be confused with that cult of suffering which is sometimes ascribed to Dostoevsky. As Lionel Trilling has argued, the underground man here is touching on a quest in which pleasure is of no use—the quest for *self-definition* and *self-affirmation*. It seeks a kind of truth that is often unpalatable; it sets "authenticity" above goodness or happiness; it reopens the question of what it means to be human and pursues the answer into dangerous and repugnant regions. This is the serious side of the underground man as paradoxalist.

But there is another side which threatens to swamp it. Paradox also signifies contradiction, real or ostensible. And the underground man is nothing if not self-contradictory. He craves isolation—and thirsts for human contact. He envies the average man—and would not be one. He rejects the laws of nature—yet explains his inertia as their inevitable product. He seeks sympathy from his reader, at the same time doing everything he can to preclude it—thus the famous pause after the opening sentence, reflecting concern lest his statement ("I am a sick man") seem a crass appeal for pity. He suffers—and proclaims his pleasure in that.

The point is that *Notes from Underground* is not at all a tract, but, as it was first announced, "A Confession." Being fired by passion, its generalizations are liable to be self-serving—and they are certain to be hyperbolic. The underground man himself insists, rightly, that they may be no less true for that. But he has also concluded that reason accounts for only one-twentieth of a human being. If we are to understand the text before us, we must accordingly attend to the other nineteen-twentieths of this character—whose corrosive intelligence, by his own admission, serves impulses for which he cannot account.

Take, for example, his often-cited arguments about freedom and individuality. He makes a brilliant case against social utopias ("the crystal palace," "the anthill," "the chicken coop") as denying "the most important and most precious thing—our personality, our individuality." And how is the latter expressed? As spontaneous desire, even caprice: "One's own free, untrammeled desires, one's own whim, no matter how extravagant, one's own fancy, be it wrought up at times to the point of madness—all of this is precisely that most advantageous of advantages which is omitted, which fits into no classification, and which is constantly knocking all the systems and theories to hell" (I, vii).

One might see the extremism of this statement as a response in kind to the extreme views the underground man is confuting (see Chernyshevsky's essay "The Anthropological Principle in Philosophy," or his novel *What Is to Be Done?*). But there are other sources for the narrator's vehemence, closer to home. He speaks of wanting to live "in order to satisfy my whole capacity for living, and not in order to fulfill my reasoning capacity alone," and he speculates that striving may be more important to man than achieving, the journey more important than arrival at the goal.

Yet how has he lived? For what has he striven? "I'll tell you solemnly that I have often wanted to become an insect. But even that wasn't granted me" (I, ii). "Perhaps the only reason I regard myself as an intelligent man is that I've never in my whole life been able either to begin or to finish anything" (I, v). "Ah, if I were doing nothing merely out of laziness! Lord, how I would respect myself then. Precisely because I would be capable at least of laziness, at least of one definite quality that I myself could be certain of" (I, vi). "I could not become anything: neither bad nor good, neither a scoundrel nor an honest man, neither a hero nor an insect. And now [at forty] I am eking out my days in my corner, taunting myself with the bitter and entirely useless consolation that an intelligent man cannot seriously become anything" (I,i).

In the absence of a character and a life—though not of the baffled appetite for both—the only constant in his existence is a morbidly sensitive self-awareness; and the unremitting content of that awareness is—pain: *Doleo, ergo sum.* His very pleasure, "strange" and "sharp," lies "precisely in this cold, loathsome half-despair, half-belief, in this deliberate burying of yourself underground for forty years out of sheer pain, in this assiduously constructed, and yet somewhat dubious hopelessness, in all this poison of unfulfilled desires turned inward, this fever of vacillations, of resolutions adopted for eternity, and of repentances a moment later" (I, iii).

The underground man, then, cultivates his pain as the one thing he has to cultivate. Suffering may be "doubt, negation," "destruction and chaos." But it is at the same time "the sole root of consciousness" (I, ix). And consciousness is for him what reverie was for Dostoevsky's dreamers of the forties, the major theater of activity and the sole sphere of freedom—only broadened by intellect and complicated by self-knowledge. Hypertrophied consciousness inhibits action, as the underground man insists; and, in a vicious circle, it goes on to usurp the place action holds in the life of the normal man. That is why he calls excessive consciousness a disease. It condemns him, for all the vitality of his mind and emotions, to life at an agonizing remove, in the form of a harangue *about* life; his preoccupations take the place of occupations; his dialogue with himself takes the place of dialogue with others, leaving him the spectator of his absent life. His own word for this condition is "underground": he listens to the life around him through a metaphoric crack in the floorboards, like an insect.

So by the end of Chapter IX, Part One, he is moved to confess that his "laws of consciousness" lead to the same lifeless state as the social ideal based on the "laws of nature" which he has been attacking. In Chapter X he evinces a frustrated desire for some alternative object of belief (we now know that the original manuscript contained hints at a Christian answer, which were unaccountably deleted by the censor). Chapter XI opens by recognizing the impasse; hesitates before it ("Hurrah for the underground! . . . To the devil with the underground!"); and turns away to confession in a new sense—via a brilliantly disarming critique:

"And isn't it disgraceful, isn't it humiliating!" you may say to me, shaking your heads in contempt.

"You long to live, yet you yourself entangle life's problems in logical confusion. And how importunate, how impudent your antics, and how frightened you are at the same time! You talk nonsense, and are pleased with it. You make insolent remarks, yet you are constantly afraid and apologetic. You insist that you fear nothing, yet at the same time you try to ingratiate yourself. You assure us that you grit your teeth, but at the same time you are trying to be witty, to make us laugh. You know that your jokes aren't witty, but you seem to be extremely pleased with their literary quality. You may, perhaps, have really suffered on occasion, but you don't have the slightest respect for your suffering. There is some truth in you, too, but no modesty; out of the pettiest vanity you bring your truth to the marketplace, you expose it to shame.... You are, indeed, trying to say something, but fear makes you reserve your final word, because you have no courage to utter it, only cowardly impertinence. You brag of your consciousness, but you merely vacillate because, though your mind works, your heart is darkened with depravity; and without a pure heart there can be no complete and true consciousness.... Lies, lies, and more lies!"

A savage and plausible indictment, but the underground man is quick to point out its insufficiency, if only on the ground that "it was I myself who just put all those words into your mouths." Now, facing the challenge that he has been avoiding some ultimate truth, he prepares to move from confession as *profession de foi* to confession as intimate reminiscence.

"Such confessions as I am about to begin here," he notes, "are not published, nor given to others to read." At the beginning (I, ii), he explained his motive for writing as a desire to understand the pleasure that accompanies degradation; thus all the ensuing speculations. But they have proved unsatisfactory; something more personal is troubling him. In resolving now "to test whether it's possible to be entirely frank at least with oneself and dare to face the whole truth," he is undertaking a kind of pre-Freudian analysis. Haunted by one particular memory, he hopes for "some relief from writing it all down." And not only relief, but perhaps even change: "Writing things down actually seems like work. They say work makes man kind and honest. Well, there's a chance, at any rate." At the end he will acknowledge failure again and call his notes "corrective punishment," but now he moves to narrative—his tale "On the Occasion of Wet Snow."

Part One has been a diffuse tirade seeking to explain and justify the "underground," a web of brilliant paradoxes fueled by pain; Part Two is a story, tracing roots of that pain in one crucial incident. Dostoevsky liked to speak of the "idea-feeling," a single entity: the two parts of *Notes from Underground* simply weight the combination on different sides. It is a brilliantly effective arrangement—first a polemic that speaks to the issues of the day but piques a curiosity about the speaker, then a "sentimental tale" about a poor clerk of the forties, seen in startling new perspective. Each would be an infinitely poorer thing without the other. (Dostoevsky frequently referred to himself as a poet, perhaps because such suggestive juxtapositions were oftener found in the poetry of his time than in fiction, with its tendency to causal explanation.)

Part Two is not only literature in a more conventional sense; it is *about* literature—in much the way that *Don Quixote* is about literature. The underground man, indeed, is a perverse descendant of the Knight of the Sorrowful Countenance; both have found in their books a life nobler and more satisfying than what the world allows, and have been possessed by it. "My chief occupation," the underground man recalls of himself at twenty, "was reading. I sought to drown all that was continually seething within me in external sensations. And the only external sensations available to me were in reading.... Aside from reading, I had nothing to turn to, nothing I could then respect in my surroundings, nothing that could attract me." In dreams he becomes a hero, and knows rapturous love. But his possession cannot be so complete as that of his great exemplar: "At times I'd get terribly tired of it." So he turns to the real world: "I longed to move about, and would suddenly plunge into dark, surreptitious, sordid debauchery—not even debauchery: mean, paltry dissipation." One activity, in fact, feeds the other—and this, he recognizes in a central insight, "is what ruined me, because, mired down in filth, I would console myself with the thought that at other times I was a hero, and the hero redeemed the filth. As if to say it would be shameful for an ordinary man to get mired down, but a hero is too sublime to be completely defiled, hence he could wallow in filth."

Only once do fantasy and actuality come together decisively—in the dramatic episode with the prostitute Liza, "dark, surreptitious debauchery" issuing suddenly (as in books!) into the possibility of compassion and perhaps love. The narrator quotes ironically from a popular poem about the redemption of just such a girl, but the irony arises only from his failure to meet the test of proffered love. Dostoevsky, by contrast, endorses the sense of the poem, taking what had become a romantic cliché and giving it a new affective validity, much as Cervantes did for some of the chivalric ideals.

"On the Occasion of Wet Snow," then, shows the underground man in the world, before his retreat to his figurative space beneath the floorboards. Much of it is comic, though with a growing admixture of pathos. Thus his stubborn desire to be thrown through a window, which leads to the elaborate pedestrian "duel" with an officer who never deigns to notice him, fought on a crowded sidewalk, with padded shoulders as weapons. When, after months of furtive preparation, the narrator does finally bump up against his antagonist, the sense of this encounter is entirely a product of his fantasy—as he all but acknowledges.

His later encounters, however, involve a more shared reality: the participants recognize him, albeit reluctantly. The path that will bring him to Liza begins with his going—out of a desperate need for human contact—to visit an old schoolmate, and involves an intensifying series of humiliations for which he bears the responsibility, not only inviting but perversely insisting on them. He is inching toward scandal, that favorite Dostoevskian device whose function is to move the action explosively forward—in this case by breaking the intolerable shell of his isolation. Scandal promises something decisive, however terrible, in the confirming presence of others. And he engineers it in the grotesquely comic scene—one of Dostoevsky's finest—at the Hotel de Paris, where a party of his old schoolmates turns into a nightmare of abasement and rejection. Nor is its meaning lost on the underground man: "So here it is, here it is at last, the confrontation with reality," he ruminates. Shamelessly cadging the fee from one of his departing schoolmates, he follows them to the brothel, filled with a sense that something irrevocable is about to happen. He is right, but the event is unexpected. Seeking compensation for the humiliations of the evening, he looses his eloquence on his companion for the night, the twenty-year-old Liza. "It's like out of a book," she recognizes—but the underground man's sole store of positive emotion is bookish, and even as he seeks to manipulate her, his own deep feeling is becoming engaged. When he urges her to quit prostitution and gives her his address, he is casting both of them in improbable roles, the roles of the speaker and the woman in the poem he quotes as epigraph. And when life has the temerity to imitate literature by bringing her to his door, his fate is sealed.

The intensity of the drama as it builds throughout this story renders comment superfluous. It has the inevitability of tragedy—though not the effect, as *Hamlet* would not if the prince escaped Rosencrantz and Guildenstern only to journey on to England, there to soliloquize until curtain-fall. The familiar dialectic repeats itself: dreams of love and glory, followed by fits of self-hatred, shame, and spite—until she comes and, weeping hysterically over the manservant who has been bullying him, he lashes her with his bitterest confession, calling himself "the vilest, the most ridiculous, the pettiest, the stupidest, the most envious of all the worms on earth," and warning: "I'll never forgive you for what I'm confessing to you now!" Liza, however, sees past his threats and insults to the unhappiness beneath, and throws her arms around his neck. Sobbing, he utters the one unqualified truth about himself. "They won't let me," he begins—and then, as if correcting himself, "I can't be . . . good!" What follows confirms this, for goodness is a part of what the underground man calls "living life," and he has already shown that he is not up to it.

On this note of painful and final recognition, the underground man moves abruptly to conclude his *Notes.* His shame in writing the story of Liza means that "this is no longer literature, but corrective punishment"—which is to say that both his covert literary aim and his avowed therapeutic aim have failed. "Because telling, for example, long tales about how I have shirked away my life through moral degeneration in my corner, through isolation from society, through loss of contact with anything alive, through vanity and malice in my underground, is really quite uninteresting. A novel requires a hero, and here there's a *deliberate* collection of all the traits for an antihero."

The antihero, however, has his legitimacy, and the underground man will not quit the stage without a last challenge to his readers: "As regards myself personally, I have in my own life merely carried to the extreme that which you have never ventured to carry even halfway; and what's more, you've regarded your cowardice as prudence, and found comfort in deceiving yourselves. So that, in fact, I may be even more 'alive' than you are. Do take a closer look! Why, we don't even know where the living lives today, or what it is, or what its name is."

The fashionable words for this state, in the late twentieth century, are alienation and anomie, and we no longer need to be persuaded that the underground man is more than an isolated case. "Either a hero or mud!" he had vowed, and proved himself the latter in the area of human relationship. But there *is* a perverse kind of heroism in this disappointed maximalist, specifically in his successful attempt to outdo Rousseau in candor, and in the perverse brilliance of his writing, which translates all the nuance of that consciousness which is—not his curse, but the symptom of his curse.

That curse is never explained in the *Notes,* nor are the materials for an explanation given. To be sure, Dostoevsky does provide in the underground man's summary of his childhood and schooling the sort of evidence that goes into the usual case history—orphanhood, poverty, emotional deprivation. But he uses such data as a decoy, a bait for shallow understandings: in fact they explain nothing. If his preexile works had shown more respect for the social and psychological as independent categories, here and henceforth they will have only ancillary value, psychological observation serving to point a metaphysical problem and the social dimension operating chiefly as an index of reality, like the solidity of the sidewalks his characters tread. In any case, he saw the posing of problems, not their solution, as his task. From *Crime and Punishment* on, the problems will be posed and explored dramatically, through shifting patterns of complex relationships, with the high seriousness of tragedy guaranteed by the finality of murder or suicide. *Notes from Underground* is unique among Dostoevsky's major works in this respect. Its protagonist cannot act—so that Raskolnikov (or any of his successors) might well turn the underground man's own words against him, claiming that "I have... in my own life, carried to the extreme that which you have never ventured to carry even halfway."

That, of course, is the sense of "underground" as the narrator uses it, for he speaks of carrying it in his soul, and claims to have inhabited it for forty years, which is to say all his life. It is the home of the "mouse," the "insect," the self-tormentor—a nagging awareness of helpless isolation from any community, a "constant and direct feeling" that only gradually has found formulation as an idea. Dostoevsky himself commented a decade later that it represented a viewpoint already transcended in his writing, but he also voiced his pride in having been the first to trace "the real man of the Russian majority" in the *Notes* and unmask his "monstrous and tragic side"—the tragedy consisting precisely in "the awareness of monstrosity." "I alone," he elaborated, "traced the tragedy of the underground, which consists in suffering, in self-punishment, in the awareness of something better, and the impossibility of attaining it—above all in the clear conviction of these unhappy people that everyone is the same and so there's no point in trying to reform! What could support those who tried to reform? Reward? Faith? There is no one to give rewards, no one to believe in. One step further and we have extreme depravity, crime (murder).... The cause of the underground is the destruction of faith in general rules. *'There is nothing sacred.'*"

This brings us back to Dostoevsky's complaints about the mutilation of his manuscript at the hands of the censor. "What is it with the censors," he wrote his brother just after the publication of Part One, "are they in a conspiracy against the government?... It would have been better not to print the penultimate chapter at all than to print it in its present form.... The censors, those swine, approved the places where I mocked everything and sometimes blasphemed *for effect,* but where I deduced the need for faith and Christ from all this—that they prohibited." Only a few cloudy hints survive in the text: "Show me something better [than the theories of Part One] and I will follow you.... I'd gladly let my tongue be cut out altogether, from sheer gratitude, if things could be arranged in such a way that I myself would never have the wish to stick it out any more.... I know myself, as clearly as two times two, that it's not at all the underground which is best, but something different, altogether different, something I long for and can never find!" (I, x).

We do not know why Dostoevsky never tried to restore the censor's cuts in subsequent editions, but it is just possible that his artist's instinct kept him from it. The baffled desire to believe, the notion of true Christianity as freedom and of true, viable individuality as Christian—these are themes that fill his later novels and require their amplitude for adequate demonstration. Simple logical deduction could hardly have led the underground man convincingly to the need for faith. (Logic, indeed, is always powerfully on the side of disbelief in Dostoevsky.) The creation of this passionate logician and anatomist of the unlived life is achievement enough, as it stands. Abrasive, unlovely, brilliant, insinuating, he commands our attention as a contemporary, posing problems as absorbing, elusive and endless as his *Notes.*

DONALD FANGER, 1974

ON THE TRANSLATION

OF ALL Russian writers, Dostoevsky is probably one of the most resistant to translation into English. The difficulty stems not only from the character of Russian as compared with English, but from the manner in which Dostoevsky used language, from the essential tenor of his writing, and the area of human experience he was concerned with.

Russian is capable of infinite emotional variation; English is more specific, more conceptual. Russian is an inflected language. By a mere change in the ending of a word, a mere flick of its tail, as it were, it can be made to express, without adjectives or articles or prepositions, a variety of qualities and relationships: not only gender, case, strength and size, but also the nuance, the degree of a given characteristic, the attitude of the author or speaker toward an object, person, or experience, and even the character of the speaker. Dostoevsky, whose prose is enormously charged emotionally, used the rich resources of the language extensively and with consummate virtuosity.

In a work as complex and as tightly woven as *Notes from Underground,* every word and every nuance is important. The translator is thus faced with the problem of transposing the text into a language which lacks many of the resources that made Dostoevsky's style so powerful and unique even in Russian, which is predicated on different assumptions—a language whose categories, especially emotional and moral categories, are often quite different. Time and again, there are no equivalents, no coincidence of values, no associative similarities; the translator must then rely on approximations and attempt to reproduce the emotional content not only by most careful word choices, but also by seeking to retain and convey, perhaps to a greater degree than is normally necessary in translation, the rhythms, the tonalities, the musical and poetic devices that carry the sense and the mood of the original.

Among its many facets, *Notes from Underground* is a satirical work (especially in the first part; the second goes beyond satire into tragic grotesque), a piece of violent self-judgment and self-flagellation both by the under-ground man, and, despite his disclaimers, by Dostoevsky himself—a kind of triple caricature: of the author, of his (and our?) "underground" aspect, and of the "men of action" whom the author and his character ridicule. There are complex layers here of irony, mockery, bitterness, hate, self-hate—and also, as in so many satires, tremendous compassion.

The narrator sees everything and everyone through savagely hostile eyes—self, associates, servants, officials, clerks, all of society, those who "walk over people" in the street and those who "duck in and out, continually stepping out of the way." Everything and everyone is reduced to a grotesque, with one exception—Liza, the meek, the wronged, the only human being in the underground man's nightmare world who is capable of love. In the passages involving her, the speaker's voice changes—there are suddenly two distinct and opposing motifs, a sudden dichotomy: "she" and "I." And whatever he does to her, in the narrative "she" is dealt with gently, with pain, compassion, and regard, while the "I" is scourged even more mercilessly than before in the narrator's agonized account of his cat-and-mouse game and the ultimate humiliation and suffering it inflicts upon her—and upon himself.

These changes in tone, these emotional subtleties and variations must be captured by the translator—by whatever verbal and nonverbal means he can command.

As always, however, translation is a struggle with impossibility, and there are losses that must be accepted as inevitable. Thus, the Russian "deyateli," which is rendered here as "men of action." The literal meaning of the word is "doer," and in Russian it is used to denote a "leading figure" active in a given field—politics, the arts, science—with the field usually specified. To the Russian reader it is entirely clear that Dostoevsky's (or his character's, for it is sometimes difficult to disentangle the author's voice from the narrator's) mockery of the obtuse, limited "doers" or "men of action" (field unspecified) is aimed primarily at the liberals, the "public citizens," the "do-gooders" of his time. This, alas, disappears in translation, unless the translator arrogates to himself the entirely inadmissible right to interpolate.

Even more regrettable is the loss of resonance between the opening line of the first part and the climactic scene of the second. "I am a sick man...I am a spiteful man..." The English "spiteful" here is a compromise solution. The Russian *zloy* includes "mean" (in its colloquial usage), "malicious," "ill-intentioned," "ill-natured," "angry," "misanthropic," "nasty," "spiteful," etc., but none of these conveys its exact meaning. And none truly resonates, as the Russian does, with the narrator's despairing cry to Liza, when she comes to him, "They won't let me...I can't be...good!" These two words, *zloy* and *dobryi* (roughly "bad" and "good"), tie the thread of self-hate and pain that runs through the entire book, closing the circle, bringing the end back to the beginning, and sealing the ultimate hopelessness. Yet the English and the Russian categories do not coincide, and a crucial element in the poetic, emotional—and philosophic—structure of the book is unavoidably shaded out.

The title itself—*Zapiski iz podpol'ya*—is another case in point. In addition to its metaphorical sense, which coincides with the English "underground," *podpol'ye* means, literally, the space "under the floor." *Notes from Underground,* then, does not convey the full connotations of the Russian title—impossible to reproduce in English.

The reader may wonder at the occasional strangeness in sentence structure, as in "An artist, let us say, has painted a picture of Ge." In dealing with such sentences, I have usually retained the equally strange form of the original.

And, finally, a word on the paragraphing. In Russian, some paragraphs run on for pages. In style, *Notes from Underground,* despite its title, is a spoken, not a written book. The breath is therefore all the more important. I broke up the extremely long paragraphs, which often obscure the complexity of meanings, into shorter ones wherever I felt that clarity demanded it, wherever I felt the speaker would have to pause.

If I have succeeded, despite all these problems, in conveying some of the quality, the undercurrents, and the tensions of the original, then the care, the pain, and the effort entailed in translating this terribly sad book will not have been in vain. But this is for the reader to judge.

I want to thank my friend Mary Mackler for reading the manuscript and offering encouragement and valuable suggestions, and Prof. Donald Fanger for his splendid introduction and his good advice on many points.

—MIRRA GINSBURG

PART ONE

UNDERGROUND*

I

I AM A SICK MAN.... I AM A SPITEFUL MAN. AN unattractive man. I think that my liver hurts. But actually, I don't know a damn thing about my illness. I am not even sure what it is that hurts. I am not in treatment and never have been, although I respect both medicine and doctors. Besides, I am superstitious in the extreme; well, at least to the extent of respecting medicine. (I am sufficiently educated not to be superstitious, but I am.) No, sir, I refuse to see a doctor simply out of spite. Now, that is something that you probably will fail to understand. Well, I understand it. Naturally, I will not be able to explain to you precisely whom I will injure in this instance by my spite. I know perfectly well that I am certainly not giving the doctors a "dirty deal" by not

*Both the author of these *Notes* and the *Notes* themselves are, of course, fictional. Nevertheless, such persons as the composer of these *Notes* not only exist in our society, but indeed must exist, considering the circumstances under which our society has generally been formed. I have wished to bring before the public, somewhat more distinctly than usual, one of the characters of our recent past. He represents a generation that is still living out its days among us. In the fragment entitled "Underground" this personage describes himself and his views and attempts, as it were, to clarify the reasons why he appeared and was bound to appear in our midst. The subsequent fragment will consist of the actual "notes," concerning certain events in his life.

Fyodor Dostoevsky

seeking treatment. I know better than anyone that I will only harm myself by this, and no one else. And yet, if I don't seek a cure, it is out of spite. My liver hurts? Good, let it hurt still more!

I have been living like this for a long time—about twenty years. Now I am forty. I used to be in the civil service; today I am not. I was a mean official. I was rude, and found pleasure in it. After all, I took no bribes, and so I had to recompense myself at least by this. (A poor joke, but I will not cross it out. I wrote it, thinking it would be extremely witty; but now I see that it was only a vile little attempt at showing off, and just for that I'll let it stand!)

When petitioners came to my desk seeking information, I gnashed my teeth at them, and gloated insatiably whenever I succeeded in distressing them. I almost always succeeded. Most of them were timid folk: naturally—petitioners. But there were also some fops, and among these I particularly detested a certain officer. He absolutely refused to submit and clattered revoltingly with his sword. I battled him over that sword for a year and a half. And finally I got the best of him. He stopped clattering. This, however, happened long ago, when I was still a young man. But do you know, gentlemen, what was the main thing about my spite? Why, the whole point, the vilest part of it, was that I was constantly and shamefully aware, even at moments of the most violent spleen, that I was not at all a spiteful, no, not even an embittered, man. That I was merely frightening sparrows to no purpose, diverting myself. I might be foaming at the mouth, but bring me a doll, give me some tea, with a bit of sugar, and I'd most likely calm down. Indeed, I would be deeply touched, my very heart would melt, though later I'd surely gnash my teeth at myself and suffer from insomnia for months. That's how it is with me.

I lied just now when I said that I had been a mean official. I lied out of sheer spite. I was merely fooling around,

both with the petitioners and with the officer, but in reality
I could never have become malicious. I was aware at every
moment of many, many altogether contrary elements. I
felt them swarming inside me, those contrary elements. I
knew that they had swarmed inside me all my life, begging
to be let out, but I never, never allowed them to come out,
just for spite. They tormented me to the point of shame,
they drove me to convulsions—I was so sick and tired of
them in the end. Sick and tired! But perhaps you think,
dear sirs, that I am now repenting of something before
you, asking your forgiveness for something?...Indeed, I
am quite certain that you think so. But then, I assure you it
doesn't make the slightest difference to me if you do....

I could not become malicious. In fact, I could not become anything: neither bad nor good, neither a scoundrel
nor an honest man, neither a hero nor an insect. And now
I am eking out my days in my corner, taunting myself
with the bitter and entirely useless consolation that an intelligent man cannot seriously become anything; that only
a fool can become something. Yes, sir, an intelligent
nineteenth-century man must be, is morally bound to be,
an essentially characterless creature; and a man of character, a man of action—an essentially limited creature.
This is my conviction at the age of forty. I am forty now,
and forty years—why, it is all of a lifetime, it is the deepest old age. Living past forty is indecent, vulgar, im-
moral! Now answer me, sincerely, honestly, who lives
past forty? I'll tell you who does: fools and scoundrels. I
will say this right to the face of all those venerable old
men, all those silver-haired, sweet-smelling old men! I
have a right to say it, because I will live to sixty myself.
To seventy! To eighty!...Wait, let me catch my
breath....

You might be imagining, gentlemen, that I am trying to
amuse you, to make you laugh? Wrong again. I am not at
all the jolly character you think I am, or may perhaps think

I am. But then, if, irritated by all this prattle (and I feel it already, I feel you are irritated), you'll take it into your heads to ask me what I am, I'll answer you: I am a certain collegiate assessor. I worked in order to eat (but solely for that reason), and when a distant relation left me six thousand rubles in his will last year, I immediately retired and settled down in my corner. I had lived here previously as well, but now I've settled down in this corner. My room is dismal, squalid, at the very edge of town. My servant is a peasant woman, old, stupid, vicious out of stupidity, and she always has a foul smell about her besides.

I am told that the Petersburg climate is becoming bad for me, that with my niggling means it's too expensive to live in Petersburg. I know all that, I know it better than all those wise, experienced counselors and head-shakers. But I stay on in Petersburg; I shall not leave Petersburg! I shall not leave because.... Ah, but what difference does it make whether I leave or don't leave.

To go on, however—what can a decent man talk about with the greatest pleasure?

Answer: about himself.

Well, then, I too shall talk about myself.

II

I WANT to tell you, gentlemen, whether you wish to hear it or not, why I was unable to become even so much as an insect. I'll tell you solemnly that I have often wanted to become an insect. But even that wasn't granted me. I swear to you, sirs, that excessive consciousness is a disease—a genuine, absolute disease. For everyday human

existence it would more than suffice to have the ordinary
share of human consciousness; that is to say, one half, one
quarter of that which falls to the lot of a cultivated man in
our wretched nineteenth century, a man who has, moreover, the particular misfortune of living in Petersburg, this
most abstract and intentional city on earth. (Cities, you
know, may be intentional or unintentional.) It would, for
instance, be quite enough to have the amount of consciousness by which all the so-called simple, direct people
and men of action live. I'll wager that you think I'm writing all this merely out of bravado, and bravado in bad taste
at that, clattering my sword like that officer, just to exercise my wit at the expense of men of action. But, my dear
sirs, who would take pride in his own diseases, and brag
about them too?

Ah, what am I saying? Everybody does it. It's precisely
their diseases that people pride themselves on, and I do—
more perhaps than anybody else. Let's not argue; my ob-
jection was absurd. But that aside, I am firmly convinced
that not only excess of consciousness, but any consciousness at all is a disease. I stand on that. However, let us
leave this for a moment, too. Tell me, now: why has it always been, as though in spite, that at the moments when I
was most capable of feeling all the refinements of "the
lofty and the beautiful,"[1] as they used to say among us
once upon a time, yes, at those very moments I . . . no, not
felt, but perpetrated such unseemly acts, such acts as . . .
well, in a word, such acts as are, perhaps, committed by
everyone, but which in my case occurred, as if on purpose,
just when I was most keenly aware that they should never
occur at all? The more aware I was of goodness and of
everything "lofty and beautiful," the deeper I sank into my
slime, and the more likely I was to get mired down in it altogether. But the main point is that all this seemed to take
place within me not by chance, but as though it had to be

so. As though this were my most normal condition rather than a disease or a corruption, so that in the end I even lost the will to fight this corruption. In the end I almost came to believe (or perhaps I really did come to believe) that this was indeed my normal condition.

And yet at first, in the beginning, how much torment I endured in this struggle! I did not think that this happened with others as well, and therefore kept it to myself all through my life as a deep secret. I was ashamed (perhaps I am still ashamed, even now). I reached a point where, trudging back to my corner on some foul Petersburg night, I would feel a certain hidden, morbid, nasty little pleasure in the acute awareness that I had once again committed something vile that day, that what had been done could no longer be undone; and I would gnaw and gnaw at myself in silence, tearing and nagging at myself until the bitterness would finally begin to turn into a kind of shameful, damnable sweetness and, in the end—into a definite, positive pleasure! Yes, a pleasure, a pleasure! I stand by that. The very reason why I brought it up is that I've always wanted to find out: do other people experience such pleasures?

I will explain it to you. This pleasure comes precisely from the sharpest awareness of your own degradation; from the knowledge that you have gone to the utmost limit; that it is despicable, yet cannot be otherwise; that you no longer have any way out, that you will never become a different man; that even if there were still time and faith enough to change yourself, you probably would not even wish to change; and if you wished, you would do nothing about it anyway, because, in fact, there is perhaps nothing to change to.

And the chief and final point is that all of this proceeds from the normal and fundamental laws of an excessive consciousness, and from the inertia which is the direct outcome of these laws; hence you not only will not change yourself, but simply cannot do a thing about it in any case. And so, in consequence of overacute consciousness, you think: that's right, you are a scoundrel—as if it were a consolation to the scoundrel to know that he is indeed a scoundrel. But enough of that.... Ah, all this twaddle, and what did I explain? What is the explanation for that pleasure? But I will explain it! I will get to the very core of it! That's what I took up the pen for....

For instance, I have a terribly sensitive ego. I am as touchy and as easily offended as a hunchback or a midget; and yet there have been moments when, if someone had slapped my face, I might have welcomed even that. I mean it: I would probably have managed to seek out a kind of pleasure even in that—naturally, it would be the pleasure of despair, but then, it's in despair that you find the sharpest pleasures, particularly when you are most acutely aware of the hopelessness of your position. And if you're slapped—why, that's when you'll be really crushed by the awareness of what muck you've been reduced to. And the main thing is that, look at it as you will, it still comes out that the fault was always yours to start with.

The worst of it, though, is that you are at fault through no fault of your own, just, so to speak, by natural law. Because, first of all, I am at fault for being more intelligent than anyone around me. (I've always considered myself more intelligent than anyone around me, and, would you believe me, I've sometimes even felt embarrassed by it. At any rate, I've always somehow looked sideways and could never look people straight in the eye.) And I'm at fault because, even if I were magnanimous, I merely would have suffered all the more from the realization of the utter uselessness of my magnanimity. For I would surely never have been able to do anything with it: neither forgive, because the man who slapped me had perhaps been prompted to it by the laws of nature, and the laws of nature are not subject to forgiveness; nor forget, for, although it's a matter of natural law, it still rankles. And, finally, even if I had wanted to be altogether ungenerous, if I had wanted to revenge myself upon the man who had insulted me, I wouldn't have been able to take revenge on anyone, since I would surely never have brought myself to do anything even if I could. Why not? That is something I want to say a few words about separately.

III

TAKE PEOPLE who know how to avenge themselves or, generally, how to stand up for themselves. How do they do it? If, let us say, they are seized with feelings of revenge, nothing exists within them at the moment except those feelings. Such a man will push on straight toward his goal like a raging bull with lowered horns, and only a wall might stop him. (Incidentally, before a wall such gentry— that is, simple, direct people and men of action—will sincerely give up. To them a wall is not a means of evasion as it would, for instance, be to us, people who think and hence do nothing; not a pretext for turning back—a pretext we ourselves don't, as a rule, believe in, but always welcome. No, they'll stop before a wall in all sincerity. A wall to them is something calming, final, morally absolving; something perhaps even mystical.... But more about walls later.)

Well, then, in my view such a direct, simple man is the true, normal human being, the kind of human being that tender mother nature herself had hoped to see when she was lovingly creating him on earth. I envy such a man to

the point of loathing. He is stupid, I admit, but perhaps a
normal man should be stupid, how do we know? Perhaps
it's even very beautiful that way. And what particularly
confirms me in this—if I may call it so—suspicion, is that
if you take, for example, the antithesis of the normal man,
that is, a man of heightened consciousness who has,
surely, emerged not from the lap of nature but from a retort
(this is almost mystical, gentlemen, but I suspect that too),
this retort-man often gives up so completely in the face of
his antithesis that he honestly feels himself, with all his
heightened consciousness, to be a mouse, not a man. He
may be an acutely conscious mouse, but a mouse all the
same, while the other is a man, and consequently . . . and so
on and so forth.

And the main thing, again, is that it's he, he himself,
who considers himself a mouse; nobody else asks him to,
and that is the important point.

Let's take a look now at this mouse in action. Let's suppose, for example, that it has also been mistreated (and it is
almost always mistreated) and also longs to avenge itself.
It will have more pent-up bitterness, perhaps, than
l'homme de la nature et de la vérité.[2] A nasty, mean little
desire to repay the offender in the same coin may be
rankling within it even more vilely than in *l'homme de la
nature et de la vérité,* because *l'homme de la nature et de
la vérité,* in his innate stupidity, views his revenge as no
more than a matter of simple justice; but the mouse, with
its heightened sensibility, denies all idea of justice as regards the situation.

And, finally, we come to the deed itself, to the act of revenge. The wretched mouse has, in addition to the first
vileness, already managed to hedge itself around with a
host of other vilenesses in the form of questions and
doubts; it has added to the one initial question so many
other unresolved questions that, willy-nilly, it will be
caught up in a fatal morass, a stinking mess consisting of

its own doubts and agitations, and, finally, of the spittle that rains upon it from the mouths of the direct men of action who solemnly stand around it as judges and arbiters, roaring with laughter at it as loudly as their healthy throats permit. Naturally, the only thing that's left to it is to shrug its little shoulders at the whole business in sheer disgust, and slip back ignominiously into its hole with a smile of feigned contempt in which it doesn't itself believe.

And there, in its loathsome, stinking underground hole, our mouse, insulted, crushed, destroyed by ridicule, immediately settles into cold, venomous, and, worst of all, life-long malice. For forty years on end it will recall its humiliation, to the last and most shameful detail, each time embellishing the recollection with still more shameful details, spitefully teasing and whipping itself up with its own fantasies. It will be ashamed of its fantasies, and yet it will recall and go over everything again and again, piling all sorts of imaginary wrongs upon itself under the pretext that they also could have happened, and never forgiving anything. It may even begin to avenge itself, but somehow in fits and starts, in trivialities, from behind the stove, as it were, incognito, without faith either in its right to vengeance or in its possible success, and knowing in advance that all of its attempts will make it suffer a hundred times more than the object of its vengeance, who may, for all you know, pay less attention to it than to a fleabite. Why, on its very deathbed the mouse will remember everything again, with all the interest accrued throughout the years, and....

But it's precisely in this cold, loathsome half-despair, half-belief, in this deliberate burying of yourself underground for forty years out of sheer pain, in this assiduously constructed, and yet somewhat dubious hopelessness, in all this poison of unfulfilled desires turned inward, this fever of vacillations, of resolutions adopted for eternity, and of repentances a moment later that you find the very essence of that strange, sharp pleasure that I spoke about. It is so subtle, so elusive, so difficult to grasp that people with the slightest limitations, or even simply those with strong nerves, will not be able to understand an iota of it. "And perhaps," you may add with a smirk, "it will not be understood by those who have never been slapped either," thus politely hinting to me that I might also have had the experience in my lifetime of being slapped and therefore speak as an expert. I'll wager that you're thinking this. But calm yourselves, gentlemen, I have not been slapped, although it is absolutely of no concern to me what you may or may not think about it. In fact, I may even regret that I have not distributed enough slaps myself in my lifetime. But enough of that, not another word about this subject, which is of such inordinate interest to you.

I will continue calmly about people with strong nerves, who do not understand certain refinements of pleasure. Although these gentry may on certain occasions, let us say, bellow like oxen at the top of their lungs, and although this is perhaps greatly to their honor, yet, as I have said before, they instantly give up in the face of impossibility. Is impossibility, then, a stone wall? What kind of a stone wall? Well, of course—the laws of nature, the conclusions of the natural sciences, mathematics. If people prove to you, for example, that you're descended from an ape,[3] there is no point in making a sour face about it; accept it as it is. If they will prove to you that, when you come down to it, one drop of your own fat is bound to be more precious to you than the lives of a hundred thousand fellow humans, and that this will in the end determine all the so-called virtues and duties and all the rest of that rot and nonsense, you have no choice but to accept it—there's nothing to be done about it, because two times two is mathematics. Try and object to that.

"For goodness sake," they'll cry, "you cannot argue against it—two times two is four! Nature doesn't consult you; it doesn't give a damn for your wishes or whether its laws please or do not please you. You must accept it as it is, and hence accept all consequences. A wall is indeed a wall...." And so on and so forth. Good God, what do I care about the laws of nature and arithmetic if, for one reason or another, I don't like these laws, including the "two times two is four"? Of course, I cannot break through this wall with my head if I don't have the strength to break through it, but neither will I accept it simply because I face a stone wall and am not strong enough.

As though such a stone wall were indeed a soothing element and really contained within itself even the slightest reason for making peace with it, solely because it means that two times two is four. Oh, absurdity of absurdities! But how preferable it is to understand everything, to be aware of everything, of all impossibilities and stone walls, and yet refuse to reconcile yourself to a single one of those impossibilities and walls if it sickens you to submit to them; how preferable to reach, by the most irrefutable logical combinations, the most revolting conclusions on the eternal subject that you are somehow to blame even for the stone wall, although, again, it is entirely obvious that you are not to blame at all; and, in consequence of all that, to sink into voluptuous inertia, silently and impotently gritting your teeth and wallowing in the idea that, as it turns out, you don't even have anyone to rail at; that you can't find any object of blame and may never find one; that all this is some sort of sleight of hand, a sharper's trick, a swindle, a plain mess in which it is impossible to tell who's who or what's what. And yet, despite all the uncertainties and confusions, you are still in pain, and the more uncertainty, the more pain!

IV

"HA-HA-HA!" YOU'LL laugh. "You will be finding pleasure in a toothache next!"

"And why not? There is pleasure in a toothache too," I'll answer. I had a toothache for a whole month. I know. In such situations, of course, people don't nurse their anger silently, they moan aloud; but these are not frank, straightforward moans, there is a kind of cunning malice in them, and that's the whole point. Those very moans express the sufferer's delectation; if he did not enjoy his moans, he wouldn't be moaning. This is a good example, gentlemen, and I'll develop it further. These moans express, to begin with, your awareness of the whole humiliating purposelessness of your pain; your recognition of the whole array of natural laws, which you, of course, don't give a hoot about, but which nevertheless make you suffer, while nature itself doesn't feel a thing. They express your realization that there is no enemy to blame, yet there is pain; that despite all the Wagenheims,[4] you are in total slavery to your teeth; that someone need only wish your toothache to stop, and it will stop, and if he doesn't wish it, the ache will go on for another three months; and, finally, that if you still refuse to submit and still go on protesting, all you can do for consolation is to give your own self a whipping or bang your fist as painfully as you can against your wall, and absolutely nothing else.

Well, then, it is these very insults, this mockery by heaven knows whom, that finally lead to a kind of pleasure which may reach the utmost heights of voluptuousness. I ask you, gentlemen, listen carefully sometimes to the moans of an educated nineteenth-century man who suffers from toothache—say, on the second or third day, when he begins to moan quite differently from the first day; that is, not simply because his teeth ache, not like some crude peasant, but like a man who has been touched by progress and European culture, a man who has "divorced himself from the soil and from the popular elements," as people say nowadays. His moans acquire a kind of nastiness, they become mean and malicious, and continue day and night. And yet he himself knows that his moans won't do him any good at all; he knows better than anyone else that he is merely lacerating and irritating both himself and others to no good purpose; he knows that even the audience, for whose benefit he is exerting himself, and his whole family are sick to death of listening to him, that they no longer believe him and know that he could moan quite differently, more simply, without all those flourishes and trills, and that he's merely indulging himself out of spite and meanness.

Well, the voluptuousness lies precisely in all these realizations, all this ignominy. As if to say, "I am disturbing you, I lacerate your hearts, I don't let anybody in the house sleep. Well then, don't sleep. I want you also to feel every moment that my teeth ache. Now I'm no longer the hero I tried to make you think I was at first, but simply a contemptible wretch, a scoundrel. All right, then! I'm delighted that you see through me. It sickens you to listen to my vile moans? Good, let it sicken you. Just wait, I'll treat you to an even nastier flourish...."

You still don't understand, gentlemen? No, it is evidently necessary to attain profounder development and deeper consciousness to understand all the complexities of this voluptuous pleasure. You're laughing? I'm delighted. My jokes, gentlemen, are certainly in bad taste, they are awkward, stumbling, full of self-distrust. But that, of course, is because I don't respect myself. Can a man of conscious intelligence have any self-respect to speak of?

V

COME NOW, can a man who has presumed to seek out enjoyment even in the very sense of his own degradation have any amount of self-respect? I am not saying this out of some mealymouthed repentance. Generally, I could never endure saying, "Forgive me, Papa, I won't do it again"—and not because I was incapable of saying it, but, on the contrary, perhaps precisely because I was all too capable of it. And how I did it! As if on purpose, I'd get myself in trouble when I hadn't done a bit of wrong. And that was the vilest part of it. Yet, again, I'd be moved to the bottom of my soul, I would repent and cry and, naturally, bluff to my own self, although I was not feigning anything at all. It was my heart that somehow got me into the mess.... Even the laws of nature could not be blamed on those occasions, though, all the same, the laws of nature have mistreated me constantly, more than anything else throughout my life. It's loathsome to recall this, and it was loathsome then as well. For after a minute or so I would already realize with anger that it was all a lie, a lie, a nauseating pretense—all that penitence, that melting heart, those vows to reform.

You may ask why I was wringing and tormenting myself like that. The answer: it was too much of a bore just to be sitting there with folded arms, and I'd start cutting up. Really, that's how it was. Try to observe your own selves more closely, gentlemen, and you will see it's so. I made up adventures, I invented a life for myself, so that at least I'd live somehow. How many times, for instance, I'd take offense, out of the blue, for no good reason, deliberately; I'd know very well that there was nothing to be offended at, that I was playacting, but in the end I'd bring myself to such a state that the offense would become real. I have been drawn to such antics all my life, till finally I no longer had any power over myself.

Or else I'd try to force myself to fall in love; in fact, I did it twice. And I suffered, gentlemen, I assure you I did. Deep down in your heart you don't believe in your suffering, there is a stirring of mockery, and yet you suffer—in the most genuine, honest-to-goodness way. I'd be jealous, I'd be beside myself.... And all out of boredom, gentlemen, all because I was crushed by sheer inertia. For the direct, inevitable, and logical product of consciousness is inertia—a conscious sitting down with folded arms. I have spoken about this before. I repeat, I repeat with emphasis: all direct and active men are active precisely because they are dull and limited. How can this be explained? Well, it's this way: because of their limitation, they mistake the most immediate and secondary causes for primary ones, and so convince themselves more quickly and more easily than others that they have found a firm, incontestable basis for their activity. This puts their minds at ease, and that, after all, is the main thing. For, naturally, to enter upon any course of action, one must be completely reassured in advance, and free of any trace of doubt. And how am I, for instance, to put my mind at ease? Where are the primary causes I can lean on, where are my basic premises? Where am I to find them? I exercise myself in thought, and hence, within my mind, every primary cause immediately drags after itself another, still more primary, and so on to infinity. Such is the very essence of all consciousness and thought. We're back, then, to the laws of nature. And what is the ultimate result? Why, the same thing again.

Remember, just a while ago I spoke about vengeance. (I doubt that you understood me.) I said that a man takes revenge because he feels it to be just. Hence, he has found a primary cause, a firm premise—namely, justice. Consequently, he is fully reassured and carries out his revenge calmly and successfully, convinced that he is performing a just and honest deed. But I see no justice in it, and no virtue; hence, if I should take revenge, it would be purely out of spite. Spite could, of course, outweigh everything, all my doubts, and thus could quite effectively take the place of a primary cause, precisely because it is not a cause. But what am I to do if there isn't even any spite in me? (And that's the point I started with just before.) With me—again because of those damned laws of consciousness—spite is also subjected to a process of chemical disintegration. And before you know it, the object disappears, arguments evaporate; no culprit is discovered, the offense ceases to be an offense and becomes a matter of fate, like the toothache which cannot be blamed on anyone, and the only thing that's left is, once again, to bang the wall as hard as you can. And you throw up your hands and give up, because you have not found a primary cause. But try and let yourself be carried away blindly by your feelings, without reflection, without a primary cause, suspending your mind at least for the moment: begin to hate or love, just so as not to sit with folded arms. The day after tomorrow, at the very latest, you'll start despising your own self because you've knowingly deceived yourself. The outcome? A soap bubble, and inertia. Why, gentlemen, perhaps the only reason I regard myself as an intelligent man is that I've never in my whole life been able either to begin or to finish anything. Call me an idle babbler if you wish, a harmless, irritating babbler, like all the rest of us. But what is to be done if the direct, the sole vocation of every intelligent man is babbling—in other words, deliberately pouring water through a sieve?

VI

AH, IF I were doing nothing merely out of laziness! Lord, how I would respect myself then. Precisely because I would be capable at least of laziness, at least of one definite quality that I myself could be certain of. Question: Who are you? Answer: A lazy man. Why, it would be a pleasure to hear this about myself. It would mean that I was positively identified, that there was something to be said about me. "A lazy man!" Why, that's a title and a vocation, it's a career. Don't joke, it's true. I would then with full right be a member of the best club, and would busily engage in the sole occupation of continually respecting myself. I knew a gentleman who prided himself throughout his life on being a connoisseur of Château Lafitte. He regarded this as a most positive virtue and never doubted himself. He died not only with a serene, but with a triumphant conscience, and he was entirely right. As for me, I would select for myself a career: I would be an idler and a glutton—and not an ordinary one, but, say, one sympathizing with everything lofty and beautiful. How do you like that? I have dreamed of it for a long time. This "lofty and beautiful" gives me a violent pain in the neck in my fortieth year. But this is my fortieth year, while then—oh, then it would have been quite different! I would immediately have found for myself an appropriate activity—namely, to drink to everything lofty and beautiful. I would have taken every possible occasion to shed a tear into my glass, then drink to everything lofty and beautiful. I would have turned everything in the world into the lofty and the beautiful. In the vilest and most ar-

rant rubbish I would have managed to discern the lofty
and the beautiful. I would have dripped tears like a wet
sponge. An artist, let us say, has painted a picture of Ge.[5]
And I would instantly drink to the health of the artist who
has painted the picture of Ge, because I love everything
lofty and beautiful. An author has written "As Anyone
Pleases";[6] and I would immediately drink the health of
"anyone," because I love everything lofty and beautiful.

And I'd demand to be respected for this, I'd persecute
those who did not show me due respect. I'd live serenely
and die with solemn dignity. But that's delightful, truly
delightful! And I would grow myself such a belly, I'd
contrive for myself such a triple chin and such a scarlet
nose that everyone I met would say, on seeing me: "Now,
that is somebody! That's somebody truly worthy and positive!" And say what you will, sirs, but it's most pleasant
to hear such comments in our negative age.

VII

BUT THESE are all golden dreams. Oh, tell me who
was the first to declare, to proclaim, that man does
vile things only because he does not realize his true interests; that if he were enlightened, if his eyes were opened to
his true, normal interests, he would immediately cease
committing abominations but would immediately become
good and noble, because, being enlightened and understanding his true advantage, he would inevitably see that
only goodness is to his advantage, and everybody knows
that no man will knowingly act against his own interests.[7]
Consequently, he would of necessity, as it were, begin to
do good. Oh, child! Oh, pure, innocent babe! Who has

ever, in all these millennia, seen men acting solely for the sake of advantage? What's to be done with the millions of facts that attest to their *knowingly*—that is, with full awareness of their true interests—dismissing these interests as secondary and rushing off in another direction, at risk, at hazard, without anyone or anything compelling them to do so, but as if solely in order to reject the designated road, and stubbornly, willfully carving out another—a difficult, absurd one—seeking it out virtually in the dark?

Evidently, then, this stubbornness and willfulness has really pleased them more than any advantage.... Advantage! What is advantage? Would you take it upon yourself to define with absolute precision where exactly man's advantage lies? And what if his advantage on a *given* occasion not only may, but must, lie exactly in choosing for himself the harmful rather than the advantageous? And if this is so, if there can be such an occasion, then the entire rule is shattered to smithereens. What do you think, can there be such an occasion? You're laughing. You may laugh, gentlemen, but answer me: have man's advantages been calculated with absolute certainty? Are there, perhaps, advantages which not only don't fit, but cannot be fitted, into any classification? After all, gentlemen, as far as I know, your entire scheme of human advantages is derived from average statistical figures and scientific-economic formulas. Your advantages are prosperity, wealth, freedom, peace of mind, and so on and so forth. So that a man who would, for instance, openly and knowingly choose to act in opposition to this whole scheme would, in your opinion—and of course in mine too—be an obscurantist or a complete madman, wouldn't he? Yet there is something astonishing about this: how is it that, in calculating man's advantages, all these statisticians, sages, and humanitarians invariably omit one of them? In fact, they don't even consider it in the form in which it should be considered, yet the entire reckoning depends on it. It would do no great harm to take this advantage and add it to the roster. But the whole trouble is that this peculiar advantage doesn't fit into any category or any scheme.

I have a friend, for example.... Ah, gentlemen! But you know him too; everybody knows him! Whenever he is about to do anything, this gentleman will immediately describe to you, clearly and eloquently, precisely how it must be done in accordance with the laws of truth and reason. More than that: he'll talk to you with fervor and passion about genuine, normal human interests. He'll ridicule nearsighted fools who do not understand either their own advantage or the true meaning of virtue. And then, exactly fifteen minutes later, without any sudden external cause, but moved by something within him that is stronger than all his interests, he'll do a turnabout, acting in total contradiction to what he himself has just been saying—against the laws of reason and against his own advantage, in short, against everything.... I will warn you that this friend of mine is a collective personage, and therefore it is rather difficult to blame him alone.

And that's just it, gentlemen. Isn't there, indeed, something that is dearer to almost every man than his very best interests, or (not to violate logic) isn't there a certain most advantageous advantage (and it's precisely the one that is omitted, the one we've mentioned just before), which is more important and more advantageous than all other advantages, and for the sake of which a man is prepared, if need be, to go against all laws, against reason, honor, peace, prosperity—in short, against all those fine and useful things—just so as to achieve this primary, this most advantageous of advantages which is more precious to him than all else?

"Well, then it's still for the sake of advantage," you'll interrupt me. Wait, we shall yet get to the point of this. Besides, it's not a matter of word play; for this advantage is remarkable precisely because it destroys all our classifications and constantly breaks down all the schemes devised by the lovers of humanity for the happiness of humankind. In short, it interferes with everything.

But before I name this advantage, I want to compromise myself personally, and will therefore impertinently declare that all these excellent schemes, all these theories about teaching mankind to understand its true, normal interests, so that, inevitably seeking to achieve these interests, it would immediately become good and noble, are for the time being—in my view—nothing but idle exercises in logic! Yes, gentlemen, exercises in logic! Why, merely to assert, say, this theory of the regeneration of mankind through the pursuit of its own advantage is, to my mind, almost like...well, like asserting with Buckle[8] that civilization makes man more gentle, and consequently less bloodthirsty and less capable of war. Logically, it might seem to follow. But man is so addicted to systems and to abstract conclusions that he is prepared deliberately to distort the truth, to close his eyes and ears, but justify his logic at all cost.

I've taken this example just because it is so vivid. Why, look around you: blood runs in rivers, and in the jolliest manner, as if it were champagne. Take this whole nineteenth century of ours, in which Buckle has also lived. Take Napoleon—both the great one, and the present one. Take North America, that eternal union.[9] Take, finally, that absurd little caricature, Schleswig-Holstein.[10] ...And what is it that civilization softens in us? Civilization merely develops man's capacity for a greater variety of sensations, and...absolutely nothing else. And, through the development of this capacity, man may yet come to find pleasure in the spilling of blood. Indeed, this has already happened. Have you noticed that the most refined bloodletters have almost all been most civilized gentlemen, beside whom the Attilas and Stenka Razins[11] often look like mere amateurs? And if they do not strike the eye as sharply as Attila and Stenka Razin, it is precisely because we see so many of them, because they are too ordinary, we've grown too accustomed to them.

In any case, if man has not become more bloodthirsty as a result of civilization, he has certainly become bloodthirsty in a nastier, uglier way than before. Before, he used to regard bloodshed as a matter of justice, and he exterminated those who had to be destroyed with a clear conscience. But today, though we regard the spilling of blood as an abomination, we still engage in this abomination, and to a far greater extent than before.

Which is worse? Decide for yourselves. It is said that Cleopatra (forgive me for taking an example from Roman history) was fond of sticking gold pins into the breasts of her slave girls and enjoyed their cries and writhings. You will say that this was, relatively speaking, in a barbarian age; that our age is also barbarian, because (again, speaking relatively) pins are also being stuck in people; that even today, though man has learned to see more clearly on occasion than he did in barbarian ages, he is still far from having *habituated himself* to behave according to the dictates of reason and science. Nevertheless, you are entirely confident that he is sure to learn, when he rids himself completely of certain of his old bad habits and when good sense and science fully reeducate human nature and direct it into normal channels. You are confident that man himself will then cease to err *voluntarily* and will, so to speak, perforce never want to set his will at variance with his normal interests. More than that: you say that then science itself will teach man (though this, to my mind, is already a luxury) that he really does not possess, and never did possess, either a will or a whim of his own; that he is, in fact, no more than a kind of a piano key or an organ stop; and that, besides, there is such a thing in the world as the laws of nature; so that everything that is done by man isn't in the least a matter of his own will, but happens of itself, according to these laws.

Consequently, all that is needed is to discover the laws of nature; then man will no longer be answerable for his actions, and life will become exceedingly easy. All human actions will, of course, be classified according to these laws—mathematically, like a logarithm table, up to 108,000—and entered in a special almanac. Or, still better, certain edifying volumes will be published, similar to our encyclopedic dictionaries, in which everything will be calculated and designated with such precision that there will no longer be any actions or adventures in the world.

And then (all this is being said by you) new economic relations will follow, ready-made and also calculated with mathematical precision, so that all possible questions will disappear in a single instant, since they will all have been provided with answers. And then the Crystal Palace will arise.[12] Then ... Well, in short, halcyon days will arrive for mankind. Of course, it is impossible to guarantee (and this, now, is myself speaking) that life will not become, let us say, dreadfully boring (for what's the point of doing anything if all is set and classified according to graphs and tables?); on the other hand, though, everything will be extremely reasonable.

Of course, who can tell what people may think up out of boredom! After all, gold pins are also stuck into bodies out of boredom. But this wouldn't be the worst of it. What's rotten (and this is again myself speaking) is that, for all we know, people might even welcome the gold pins. For man is stupid, phenomenally stupid. Well, perhaps not stupid at all, but ungrateful, so ungrateful that you wouldn't find another like him. For example, I would not be in the least surprised to see a certain gentleman get up, out of the blue, in the midst of the general future reign of reason, with an ignoble—or, better, with a retrograde and mocking—physiognomy, and say to us, with his arms akimbo: "What, my dear sirs, if we should smash all this good sense to smithereens with one hard kick, to the sole end of sending all these logarithms to the devil and living a while again according to our own stupid will!" And even this wouldn't be so bad. What really hurts is that he would unquestionably win followers: that's how man is constituted. And all for the most trifling reason, which hardly seems worth mentioning: namely, that man, whoever he might be, has always and everywhere preferred to act according to his own wishes rather than according to the dictates of reason and advantage. And his wishes may well be contrary to his advantage; indeed, sometimes they *positively should be* (this, now, is my idea).

One's own free, untrammeled desires, one's own whim, no matter how extravagant, one's own fancy, be it wrought up at times to the point of madness—all of this is precisely that most advantageous of advantages which is omitted, which fits into no classification, and which is constantly knocking all systems and theories to hell. And where did our sages get the idea that man must have normal, virtuous desires? What made them imagine that man must necessarily wish what is sensible and advantageous? What man needs is only his own *independent* wishing, whatever that independence may cost and wherever it may lead. And the devil knows what this wishing. . . .

VIII

H A-HA-HA!" YOU interrupt me, roaring with laughter. "But, if you don't mind, there isn't even such a thing as wishing! Science has managed by now to anatomize man to such a degree that we already know that all your wishing, your so-called free will is nothing but . . ."

Wait, gentlemen, this is what I intended to begin with myself. In fact, you've startled me for a moment. I was just about to exclaim that the devil alone knows what this wishing depends on, and that perhaps we ought to thank God for that, when I remembered science, and...broke off. And here you've brought it up. And indeed, if someday they should really discover the formula for all our whims and wishes—I mean, what causes them, what laws they're governed by, how they develop and where they lead in one case or another, and so on and so forth; in other words, an actual mathematical formula—why, then man will perhaps immediately stop wishing; indeed, he'll surely stop wishing. Who wants to wish according to graphs? Besides, man will at once be turned into an organ stop or some such thing, for what is man without desires, without will or wishes, if not a mere stop in some organ or other? What do you think? Let's consider the probabilities— can such a thing happen, or can't it?

Hm...you decide. Our wishes are mostly wrong and mostly due to a mistaken conception of our advantage. We often want sheer nonsense because, in our stupidity, we see this nonsense as the easiest path to the achievement of some supposed advantage. But when all this is explained and worked out on a piece of paper (which is entirely possible, for it would be vile and senseless to believe in advance that there are certain natural laws which man will never learn), then, of course, there will be no more so-called desires. For if desires are one day brought into complete accord with reason, then we shall reason instead of wishing. After all, it is impossible, while you retain your sanity, to *wish* nonsense and go deliberately against reason by choosing what is harmful to you....

And since all wishing and reasoning can actually be tabulated, because one day the laws that govern our so-called free will are bound to be discovered, then—all jokes aside—some sort of graph will be drawn up, so that we shall indeed be wishing according to this graph. For, let us say, if some day they will calculate and prove to me that, if I stuck my tongue out at someone, it was because I could not help but do it, and that I inevitably had to stick it out precisely to a certain length, then what remains to me of *freedom,* especially if I'm an educated man and have completed a course of studies at some school? Why, in that case I should be able to calculate my whole life in advance for thirty years! In short, if that is how it will be, there will be nothing left for us to do; we shall have to accept whatever comes. And besides, we must tirelessly repeat to ourselves that, at any given moment and in any given circumstances, nature won't trouble to consult us; that it must be accepted as it is, and not as we imagine it. And if we really aspire to graphs and schedules, and even . . . even perhaps to a retort as well, then there's no help for it—we must accept the retort too! For it will get itself accepted, with or without our consent. . . .

Ah, but there's the rub! Forgive me, gentlemen, for all my philosophizing—it's my forty years underground! Allow me to indulge my fancy. You see, gentlemen, reason is unquestionably a fine thing, but reason is no more than reason, and it gives fulfillment only to man's reasoning capacity, while desires are a manifestation of the whole of life—I mean the whole of human life, both with its reason and with all its itches and scratches. And though our life in these manifestations will often turn out a pretty sorry mess, it is still life and not a mere extraction of square roots. After all, I quite naturally want to live in order to fulfill my whole capacity for living, and not in order to fulfill my reasoning capacity alone, which is no more than some one-twentieth of my capacity for living. What does reason know? It knows only what it has managed to learn (and it may never learn anything else; that isn't very reassuring, but why not admit it?), while human nature acts as a complete entity, with all that is in it, consciously or unconsciously; and though it may be wrong, it's nevertheless alive.

I suspect, gentlemen, that you look upon me with pity. You repeat to me that an educated and enlightened man— in short, man as he will be in the future—cannot knowingly desire something disadvantageous to himself; that this is mathematics. I entirely agree—it is indeed mathematics. But I repeat to you for the hundredth time: there is only one occasion, one only, when man may purposely, consciously choose for himself even the harmful and the stupid, even the stupidest thing—just so that he will *have the right* to wish the stupidest thing, and not be bound by the duty to have only intelligent wishes. For this most stupid thing, this whim of ours, gentlemen, may really be more advantageous to us than anything on earth, especially in certain cases. In fact, it may be the most advantageous of all advantages even when it brings us obvious harm and contradicts the most sensible conclusions of our reason concerning our advantage. Because, at any rate, it preserves for us the most important and most precious thing—our personality, our individuality.

There are people who assert that this is indeed the most precious thing to man. Of course, wishing may, if it chooses, coincide with reason, especially if this isn't overdone but used in moderation; that is both beneficial and, at times, even praiseworthy. But desires will often—indeed, in most cases—stubbornly and directly contradict reason, and . . . and . . . and do you know, gentlemen, that too is beneficial and even highly praiseworthy at times.

Let us suppose, gentlemen, that man is not stupid. (And really, you cannot say he is stupid, if only for the reason that if he is stupid, then who is intelligent?) But even if he isn't stupid, he is nevertheless monstrously ungrateful! Phenomenally ungrateful! I even think that the best definition of man is: a biped, ungrateful. But this isn't all; this is not yet his principal fault; his chiefest fault is his constant

depravity—constant, from the time of the Universal
Deluge to the Schleswig-Holstein period of human destiny. Depravity, and hence lack of good sense. For it has
long been known that lack of good sense results from
nothing other than depravity. Just glance at the history of
mankind. What will you see? A grandiose spectacle?
Perhaps. Think of the Colossus of Rhodes—that alone is
surely worth something! No wonder Mr. Anayevsky[13] at-
tests that some people say it is the product of human
hands, while others insist that it is the creation of nature itself. Colorful? Perhaps that, too. Take just the gala uniforms, military and civilian, of all the peoples of all
times—aren't they something! And if you add the regular
uniforms of civilian officials—why, you can break a leg
trying to sort them out. No historian could keep up with
them. Monotonous? Well, perhaps monotonous too: fighting and fighting; fighting today, and fighting in the past,
and fighting again afterwards. You must agree it's really
altogether too monotonous.

In short, anything can be said about world history, anything that might occur to the most distraught imagination.
There is only one thing that cannot be said about it—that it
is sensible. Why, the very word will stick in your throat.

And then there is this curious thing that you encounter
every minute: you constantly come up in life against those
virtuous and sensible people, sages and lovers of mankind,
who make it their very life's purpose to conduct themselves at all times as properly and sensibly as possible; to
serve, as it were, as guiding lights to their fellow men, to
the end of proving to them that it is indeed possible to live
in the world both decently and sensibly. And what does it
all come down to? We know how many of these lovers of
mankind have sooner or later ended up by betraying their
own fine principles and pulling some scandalous antic—
often of a most disreputable nature.

And now I'll ask you: what can be expected of man, a

creature endowed with such strange qualities? Why, shower him with every earthly good, drown him in happiness over his head, so that only bubbles will spring up on the surface of this happiness, as on water; give him such economic prosperity that he'll have nothing left to do but sleep, eat pastries, and busy himself with assuring the continuance of world history. And even then, out of sheer ingratitude, sheer nastiness, he will commit some vileness. He'll even risk his pastries and deliberately choose the most pernicious nonsense, the most uneconomical absurdity—solely in order to inject his noxious fantastic element into all that positive, sensible bliss. He will insist on clinging precisely to his own fantastic dreams, his most vulgar folly, solely in order to confirm to himself (as if this were, indeed, so necessary) that men are still men, and not piano keys, which may be played by the hands of natural laws themselves, but which are threatened by this very playing to be brought to a state where it will no longer be possible to wish a thing outside of graphs and schedules. But even that isn't all. Even in case he really might turn out to be nothing but a piano key, and even if this were proved to him by the natural sciences and mathematics, man still won't come to his senses, and will do something deliberately contrary, solely out of ingratitude, and to insist on his own way.

And if he should lack the means to do so, he will invent destruction and chaos, he will invent a variety of sufferings, and will have his own way, no matter what! He will unleash a curse upon the world, and since only man is capable of cursing (that's his privilege and his chief distinction from other animals), he will, perhaps, attain his end just by his cursing; in other words, he will prove to himself that he is a man, and not a piano key! If you will say that all this—the chaos, and the darkness, and the curse—can be calculated according to a table, so that the very possibility of advance calculation will stop it all, and reason will

retain the upper hand, then man will deliberately go insane
for the occasion, in order to have no reason and still get his
way! I believe this, I vouch for it, because all of man's purpose, it seems to me, really consists of nothing but proving
to himself every moment that he is a man and not an organ
stop! Proving it even at the cost of his own skin; even at the
cost of turning back into a troglodyte. And after that, how
can one resist the temptation of boasting that it still isn't
so, that man is still not a piano key, that human desires still
depend on the devil knows what. . . .

You shout to me (if you still deign to shout to me) that
nobody is depriving me of will; that the only thing in question is to arrange things in such a way that my will itself,
by its own free will, shall coincide with my normal interests, with the laws of nature, with arithmetic.

Ah, gentlemen, what kind of independent will can there
be when it comes down to graphs and to arithmetic, when
nothing counts but "two times two makes four"? Two
times two will be four even without my will. Is that what
you call man's free will?

IX

O F COURSE, I am joking, gentlemen, and I know
myself that it's a poor joke, but after all, not everything is to be taken as a joke. I may be gritting my teeth as
I joke. Gentlemen, I am tormented by questions; answer
them for me. Here, for example, you are trying to cure man
of old habits and correct his will according to the demands
of science and good sense. But how do you know that
man not only can, but indeed *should* be remade in this
manner? What makes you think that human desires *must*

be corrected? In short, how do you know that such correction will really be to man's advantage? And, to be altogether frank, why are you so *absolutely* convinced that not going against true, normal advantages, guaranteed by reason and arithmetic, is really always to man's advantage, and is a law for all mankind? After all, for the time being this is no more than your hypothesis. Suppose it is a law of logic, but not a law of mankind at all? You may be thinking, gentlemen, that I'm a madman. Let me explain myself. I agree—man is primarily a creative animal, condemned to strive consciously toward a goal and to engage in the engineering arts; in other words, to be eternally and continually building roads for himself, leading *somewhere, no matter where.* But he may sometimes be tempted to slip off to the side precisely because he is *condemned* to build these roads, and also perhaps because, despite the general stupidity of the direct man of action, it nevertheless occurs to him now and then that the road, after all, almost always leads *somewhere, no matter where,* and that the main thing isn't where it leads, but just that it leads and that the well-behaved child should not, disdaining the engineering arts, lapse into pernicious idleness which, as everybody knows, is the mother of all vices.

Man loves to create, and to build roads. That is beyond question. But why, then, does he also passionately love destruction and chaos? Tell me that! But this is something I want to say two words about separately myself. Can it be that he is so dedicated to destruction and chaos (and it's unquestionable that he is at times extremely dedicated to it, that's a fact), because he is himself instinctively afraid of achieving his goal and completing the edifice he is constructing? How do you know, perhaps he loves the edifice only from afar, and not at all at close range; perhaps he only loves to build it, and not to live in it, leaving it afterwards *aux animaux domestiques,* such as ants, sheep, and so on, and so forth. Now ants have altogether different tastes. They have a remarkable edifice of a similar type, forever immutable—the anthill.

The estimable ants began with the anthill, and they will probably end with the anthill, which does great honor to their consistency and trustworthiness. But man is a flighty, deplorable creature, and, like a chess player, he may be fond only of the process of achieving the goal, rather than of the goal itself. And who knows (no one can vouch for that), perhaps the only goal toward which mankind is striving on earth consists of nothing but the continuity of the process of achieving—in other words, of life itself, and not the goal proper, which, naturally, must be nothing but two times two is four—in other words, a formula; and two times two, gentlemen, is no longer life, but the beginning of death.

At any rate, man has always somehow feared this two times two makes four. And I still fear it. Granted that man does nothing but search out those two times two makes four; he sails across oceans, he sacrifices his life in this quest, but, I would swear, he's somehow afraid of really finding, discovering it. For he feels that, as soon as he finds it, there will be nothing to search for. Workmen, at least, will get their wages when they finish work, go to a tavern, then end up in the precinct house—and there's a full week's occupation. But where is man to go? At any rate, you see a kind of embarrassment in him whenever he achieves a certain goal. He is fond of striving toward achievement, but not so very fond of the achievement itself, and this is, naturally, terribly funny. In short, man is constructed comically; there is evidently some joke in all of this. But two times two makes four is still an altogether insufferable thing. Two times two makes four—why, in my view, it is sheer impertinence. Two times two makes four is a brazen fop who bars your way with arms akimbo, spitting. I agree that two times two makes four is an excellent thing; but if we are dispensing praise, then two times two makes five is sometimes a most charming little thing as well.

And why are you so firmly, so solemnly convinced that only the normal and the positive—in short, only well-being—is to man's advantage? What if reason should err in its judgment of advantages? After all, man may be fond not only of well-being. Perhaps he is just as fond of suffering? Perhaps suffering is just as much in his interest as well-being? And man is sometimes extremely fond of suffering, to the point of passion, in fact. And here there is no need to consult world history; ask your own self, if you're a man and have lived at all. As for my personal opinion, it's even somehow indecent to love only well-being. Whether it's good or bad, smashing something is also very pleasant on occasion.

Actually, I hold no brief for suffering, nor am I arguing for well-being. I argue for . . . my own whim, and the assurance of my right to it, if need be. In vaudeville, for instance, suffering is inadmissible, I know that. In a crystal palace it's unthinkable; suffering is doubt, negation, and what kind of a crystal palace would it be if doubt were possible in it? And yet I am convinced that man will never give up true suffering—that is, destruction and chaos. Why, suffering is the sole root of consciousness. Though I declared in the beginning that consciousness, in my view, is man's greatest misfortune, I know that man loves it and will never exchange it for any satisfactions. Consciousness, for example, is infinitely nobler than two times two. After two times two, there would be nothing left, not only to do, but even to learn. The only thing possible then would be to stop up your five senses and submerge yourself in contemplation. And though with consciousness you reach the same result—a state in which there's nothing to be done—at least you can then whip yourself from time to time, and this, at any rate, is somewhat enlivening. Retrograde, yes, but still better than nothing.

X

YOU BELIEVE in a crystal edifice, eternal and imperishable, an edifice at which one never can stealthily stick out his tongue or make a fist, even in one's pocket. As for me, I am perhaps afraid of this edifice just because it is crystal and forever imperishable, and because it will be impossible even stealthily to stick out a tongue at it.

You see, if there should be a chicken coop instead of your palace, and it begins to rain, I may crawl into this chicken coop to avoid getting wet; yet I will not imagine that this chicken coop is a palace out of gratitude, because it gave me shelter from the rain. You are laughing, you even say that in such a case a chicken coop and a mansion are the same. Surely—I answer you—if the sole purpose of living is to keep from getting wet.

But what is to be done if I have taken it into my head that this is not the only purpose in life, and that, if you're to live at all, it's best to live in a mansion? This is my wish, my desire. You can scrape it out of me only if you alter my desires. Well, then, alter them, tempt me with something else, give me another ideal. But until then I will not take a chicken coop to be a palace. Let's even suppose that the crystal edifice is a figment of the imagination, that the laws of nature preclude it, that I've invented it merely out of my own stupidity, as a result of certain antiquated, irrational habits of our generation. Yet what do I care if it's precluded? What difference does it make, if it exists in my desires, or, to put it more exactly, if it exists while my desires exist?

Are you laughing again? Laugh if you wish; I will accept all ridicule, and yet I will not say I'm full when I am hungry. I still know that I will not reconcile myself to a compromise, to an endlessly recurring zero, simply because it exists according to the laws of nature, and exists in *reality*. I will not accept as the crown of my aspirations a solidly built house with apartments for the poor, leased for a thousand years, and provided, for any eventuality, with the dentist Wagenheim on a signboard. Destroy my desires, eradicate my ideals, show me something better, and I will follow you. You may say I'm not worth bothering with; in that case, I can say exactly the same to you. We are talking seriously. And if you do not deign to give me your attention, I will not bow before you. I have my underground.

But while I am still alive and have desires—why, may my arm wither if I contribute even a single little brick to such a solid building! Never mind that I have just rejected the crystal edifice, for the sole reason that one will not be able to stick out a tongue at it. I said that not at all because I am so fond of sticking out my tongue. Perhaps the reason I was angry was merely that, of all your buildings, there is still none at which one is not tempted to stick out his tongue. On the contrary, I'd gladly let my tongue be cut out altogether, from sheer gratitude, if things could be arranged in such a way that I myself would never have the wish to stick it out any more. What do I care if this is impossible to arrange, and we are expected to content ourselves with apartments? Why, then, was I endowed with such desires? Can it be that I was made this way simply so that I'd come to the conclusion that my whole way of being is nothing but a fraud? Can this be the sole purpose of it? I don't believe it.

But do you know what? I am convinced that we underground men must be kept well reined in. A man like me may be capable of sitting in his hole for forty years with-

out a word, but once he comes outside and breaks out into
speech, he'll talk and talk and talk. . . .

XI

AND IN conclusion, gentlemen, the best thing is to do
nothing! The best thing is conscious inertia! And so,
hurrah for the underground! Though I have said that I envy
the normal man to the point of the bitterest gall, yet, under
the conditions in which I see him, I do not want to be one.
(Though, all the same, I shall not cease to envy him.) No,
no, the underground is, at any rate, more advantageous!
There, at least, one can... Ah, but I'm lying again! Lying,
because I know, as clearly as two times two, that it's not at
all the underground which is best, but something different,
altogether different, something I long for and can never
find! To the devil with the underground!

In fact, the best thing would be this: if I myself believed
at least a jot of what I have just written. I swear to you,
gentlemen, I don't believe a single word, not one, of what
I've scribbled just now! That is, I do, perhaps, believe it,
yet at the same time, heaven knows why, I have a feeling, a
suspicion that I'm lying like a cobbler.

"Why, then, did you write all this?" you'll ask me.

Well, suppose I had shut you up for forty years without
a thing to do, then came to you, in your underground hole,
after forty years to see what had become of you? Is it right
to leave a man alone for forty years without anything
to do?

"And isn't it disgraceful, isn't it humiliating!" you may
say to me, shaking your heads in contempt. "You long to
live, yet you yourself entangle life's problems in logical

confusion. And how importunate, how impudent your antics, and how frightened you are at the same time! You talk
nonsense, and are pleased with it. You make insolent remarks, yet you are constantly afraid and apologetic. You
insist that you fear nothing, yet at the same time you try to
ingratiate yourself. You assure us that you grit your teeth,
but at the same time you are trying to be witty, to make us
laugh. You know that your jokes aren't witty, but you seem
to be extremely pleased with their literary quality. You
may, perhaps, have really suffered on occasion, but you
don't have the slightest respect for your suffering. There is
some truth in you, too, but no modesty; out of the pettiest
vanity you bring your truth to the marketplace, you expose
it to shame.... You are, indeed, trying to say something,
but fear makes you reserve your final word, because you
have no courage to utter it, only cowardly impertinence.
You brag of your consciousness, but you merely vacillate
because, although your mind works, your heart is darkened with depravity; and without a pure heart there can be
no complete and true consciousness. And how importunate you are, how you beg attention, how you clown! Lies,
lies, and more lies!"

Of course, it was I myself who just put all these words
into your mouths. This, too, is from the underground. I've
been sitting there for forty years and listening to these
words of yours through a crack in the floor. I have invented
them myself, for nothing else would come into my mind.
No wonder I've learned them by heart, no wonder they
have taken literary form....

But you, are you really so gullible as to imagine that I
will publish all of this, and let you read it, too? And here's
another problem: why do I keep addressing you as "gentlemen," why do I speak to you as though you were actually
my readers? Such confessions as I am about to begin here
are not published, nor given to others to read. At least, I
don't possess sufficient fortitude to do it, and don't see

why I should possess it. But, you see, a certain fancy has come into my mind, and I want to realize it at any cost. The point is this:

In every man's memory there are things he won't reveal to others, except, perhaps, to friends. And there are things he won't reveal even to friends, only, perhaps, to himself, and then, too, in secret. And finally, there are things he is afraid to reveal even to himself, and every decent man has quite an accumulation of them. In fact, the more decent the man, the more of them he has stored up. At any rate, I have myself only recently gotten up the courage to recall some of my former adventures, which up until now I have always skirted—indeed, with a kind of anxiety. But now, precisely now, when I have not only recalled them but have even decided to write them down, I want to test whether it's possible to be entirely frank at least with oneself and dare to face the whole truth. Incidentally, Heine says that true autobiographies are almost impossible, that man is sure to lie about himself. He is certain, for example, that Rousseau had lied about himself in his confessions—had lied, in fact, deliberately, out of vanity.

I am sure that Heine is right. I understand very well how it is possible sometimes to slander yourself, to admit to all sorts of crimes solely out of vanity, and I have a very clear idea of what such vanity can be like. But Heine spoke about the man who made his confession in public. I, on the other hand, am writing for myself alone, and declare once for all that, even if I write as though I were addressing readers, I do it merely for form's sake, because it is easier for me to write like that. It's nothing but a device, an empty device. As for readers, I will never have any. I have already said so.

I don't want to restrict myself in any way by editing my notes. I will not attempt any order or method. I will write down whatever comes to mind.

Now, for example, someone might try to catch me at

my word and ask: If you really expect no readers, why are you setting up conditions for yourself, and on paper, too—promising that you will attempt no order or method, that you will write down whatever comes to mind, and so on, and so forth? Why all these explanations? Why the apologies?

"Well," I'll answer, "that's how it is."

There is, incidentally, a whole psychology in this. Perhaps, too, the answer is that I'm simply a coward. Or that I'm purposely imagining an audience so as to behave more decently while I am writing. There may be a thousand reasons.

And also this: why, actually, do I want to write at all? If not for an audience, then couldn't I simply go over everything just in my mind, without putting it on paper?

Right enough. Yet it will somehow be more solemn when put down on paper. There's something more impressive about it, there will be more judgment of myself, it will be in better style. Besides, I may in fact get some relief from writing it all down. Today, for instance, I am particularly oppressed by a certain memory of long ago. It came to my mind vividly the other day, and ever since then it has stayed with me like an annoying tune that won't leave you alone. And yet you must get rid of it. I have hundreds of such memories; but at times one will come up out of the hundreds and oppress me. For some reason I think that it will leave me alone once it is written down. Why not try, then?

Lastly, I am bored, and I never do anything. And writing things down actually seems like work. They say work makes man kind and honest. Well, there's a chance, at any rate.

It's snowing now, an almost wet snow, yellow, murky. Yesterday it snowed too, and the day before. I think it is this wet snow that recalled to me the incident that now refuses to let me rest. And so, let this be a tale on the occasion of wet snow.

PART TWO

ON THE OCCASION OF WET SNOW

When from the darkness of delusion
With ardent words of persuasion
I drew your fallen soul to light,
And, heart rent with profound torment,
Wringing your hands you cursed the vice
That held you captive in its snares;
When, punishing by recollection
Your conscience that had slept so long,
You led me through the sordid tale
Of all the years before we met,
And suddenly your face you covered,
With utter shame and horror filled,
Venting your grief in bitter tears,
Revolted, shaken to your depths....
Etc., etc., etc.

FROM A POEM BY N. A. NEKRASOV[14]

I

I WAS ONLY TWENTY-FOUR AT THE TIME. MY life was already then gloomy, disorderly, and wildly solitary. I did not associate with anyone, avoiding even conversations, and retreated more and more into my corner. At work, in the office, I tried not to look at anyone, and I was perfectly aware that my colleagues not only considered me an eccentric, but—I felt that too—seemed to regard me with a kind of loathing. Sometimes I wondered: why didn't anyone else think that people regarded him with loathing? why was I the only one who thought so? One of our clerks had a repulsive pockmarked face—the face, I'd even say, of a brigand. I think I wouldn't have dared to look at anyone, with such an indecent face. Another wore a uniform so old and greasy that he smelled. Yet neither of these gentlemen showed any embarrassment—over his clothes, or face, or moral qualities. Neither one nor the other imagined that he was regarded with loathing; and even if they had imagined it, they wouldn't have cared, as long as it wasn't their superiors who chose to view them in this manner.

Today it is entirely clear to me that, due to my unbounded vanity and hence demands upon myself, I often looked upon myself with furious dissatisfaction, verging on loathing, and therefore mentally attributed my own feeling to others. For example, I hated my face. I thought it was revolting and even suspected that it bore a kind of nasty, abject expression; and therefore every time I came to work I painfully tried to carry myself as independently as possible and to assume the noblest air, so that no one would suspect me of abjectness. It may not be a handsome face, I thought, but let it be nobly expressive and, above all, *extremely* intelligent. But I knew with agonizing certainty that my face would never express all these perfections. Worst of all, I found it positively stupid. And I would gladly have settled just for intelligence. I even would have reconciled myself to an abject expression if only people would at the same time find my face terribly intelligent.

Naturally, I detested all my office colleagues, down to the last one, and despised them all, and yet I seemed to fear them too. At times I'd even suddenly decide they were superior to me. In those years my feelings were always shifting suddenly: now I despised people, now set them above myself. A cultivated and decent man cannot be vain without making boundless demands upon himself and without moments of self-contempt verging on self-hatred. But whether I despised a man or felt he was superior, I almost always dropped my eyes before his. I even made experiments: could I endure the glance of this one or that one? And always I was the first to drop my eyes. This tormented me to the point of rage. I was also morbidly afraid of looking ridiculous and therefore slavishly worshiped established conventions in everything external; I set myself with dedication into the general groove and deeply dreaded any sign of eccentricity within me.

Yet how could I sustain this? I was morbidly developed, as a cultivated man of our age must be. And they were all dull-witted, and as like one another as sheep in a flock. I was perhaps the only man in our office who constantly thought himself a coward and a slave; I thought so precisely because I was cultivated. But I not only thought so. It was true in fact: I was a coward and a slave. I say this without any embarrassment. Every decent man of our time is and is bound to be a coward and a slave. This is his normal condition. I am deeply convinced of that. This is how he is constituted, and this is what he is meant to be. And not only today, as a result of some chance circumstances; no, a decent man has generally and at all times had to be a coward and a slave. This is a law of nature for all decent men on earth. And if one of them happens to show a bit of courage in some situation, he needn't take comfort or get carried away by it; he will be sure to back down in the face of something else. That's how it eternally and invariably ends up. Only asses and their mongrel hangers-on will flaunt their courage, and even then only until they reach that certain wall. But why waste time on them, they're absolutely of no consequence.

Another thing tormented me in those days: the fact that no one else was like me, and I was like no one else. I am alone, I thought, and they are *everybody*. And I worried about it.

That goes to show how young I was.

I'd also fall into opposite extremes. I'd loathe going to the office so much that I would often come home sick. Then suddenly, out of nowhere, would come a phase of skepticism and indifference (everything in my life came in phases), and I myself would begin to mock my own intolerance and squeamishness, accusing myself of *romanticism*. Either I wouldn't want to talk to any of my colleagues, or else I'd get into a talking streak and even take it into my head to make friends with them. For no apparent reason, all my squeamishness would suddenly disappear. Who knows, perhaps I never felt it at all, perhaps it was all pretense, picked up from books. I haven't answered that question to this very day. At one time I even became altogether chummy with them, began to visit them at their homes, play preference,[15] drink vodka, discuss office affairs and promotions.... But permit me now to digress a bit.

We Russians, generally speaking, have never had any stupid transmundane romantics of the German and, especially, the French variety, whom nothing ever affects: the earth might be cracking beneath them, all of France might be perishing on the barricades, yet they remain the same. They wouldn't change even for decency's sake. They'll go on singing their starry tunes, so to speak, to their dying day, because they're fools. But in our country, in Russia, there are no fools. This is a known fact. This is what makes us different from all those foreign German lands. Consequently, we have no starry natures in pure, unadulterated form. That's all a fiction, invented by our "positive" publicists and critics of that period, who hunted out the Kostanzhoglos and the Uncle Pyotr Ivanoviches[16] whom, in their folly, they set up as our ideal; at the same time they slandered our romantics, assigning them to the same transmundane breed as the Germans and the French. On the contrary, our romantics are the absolute and direct opposite of the starry Europeans, and none of your little European yardsticks will fit here. (I trust you will allow me to use the term "romantic"—a good old word, esteemed and honored and familiar to all.)

Our romantic understands everything, *sees everything, and sees it often far more clearly than our most positive, practical minds*. He reconciles himself to nothing and no one, but at the same time will not spurn anything; he'll sidestep everything, yield on every point, treat everybody with politic tact; he'll never lose sight of useful, practical objectives (say, an apartment at government expense, a pension, a decoration, a medal)—and he will keep an eye on these objectives through all his enthusiasms and little volumes of lyrical verse. At the same time he will to his dying breath preserve inviolate his vision of "the lofty and the beautiful" and, while he is at it, preserve himself as well, wrapped tenderly in cotton wool like a bit of precious jewelry—again, perhaps, for the sake of that "lofty and beautiful" vision of his.

He's a man of breadth and scope, our romantic, and the greatest fraud of all our frauds. I assure you of that.... In fact, I assure you of that from experience. Of course, all this is so if the romantic is clever. But what am I saying! The romantic is always clever. What I meant was that, although we've had some romantic fools, those do not count, simply because they would degenerate completely into Germans while still in their prime, and, the more comfortably to preserve their bit of jewelry, they'd settle somewhere way out there, mostly in Weimar or in Schwarzwald.

I, for instance, sincerely despised my work, and if I didn't spit at it, it was purely out of necessity, because I myself sat in that office and was paid for it. Still—you will note—I didn't spit. Our romantic would sooner lose his mind (which, however, happens very seldom) than spit when he has no other career in prospect; and he won't let himself be pushed out, either, unless he's taken to the madhouse as "the King of Spain,"[17] and even then only if his madness becomes altogether too extreme. But in our country it's only the seedy ones, with the pale, sandy hair who lose their minds, while countless romantics attain considerable rank as time goes on. What admirable versatility! And what capacity for the most contradictory emotions! I took comfort in this even in those early years, and, indeed, am of the same view today. This is why we have so many "broad, generous natures" who never give up their ideal, no matter how low they might sink. And though they will not raise a finger for that ideal, though they may be the most outrageous rogues and thieves, they nevertheless are moved to tears by their original ideal, and are extraordinarily honorable deep in their hearts. Oh, yes, it is only in our midst that the most arrant scoundrel can be completely and even nobly honest at heart while never for a moment ceasing to be a scoundrel. Let me repeat: think how often we see our romantics turn into the shrewdest rascals (and I use the term "rascals" affectionately), suddenly displaying such a nose for reality, such a positive sense of the expedient, that their stunned superiors and the general public only cluck their tongues in amazement.

Their versatility is truly remarkable, and God knows what turn it will take and how it will develop in time to come, or what it promises us in our future. Oh yes, they're splendid material! And I'm not saying this out of some ridiculous, exaggerated patriotism. However, I'm sure you are imagining again that I am joking. Or, perhaps—quite on the contrary—you're certain that I really mean this. In any case, gentlemen, I will consider either view as an honor and a particular pleasure. As for my digression, I trust you will forgive it.

Naturally, my friendships with my colleagues did not last; very soon I'd quarrel with them and, owing to the inexperience of youth, I'd even stop greeting them, as though I had cut them off entirely. This, however, happened to me only once. In general I was always alone.

My chief occupation at home was reading. I sought to drown all that was continually seething within me in external sensations. And the only external sensations available to me were in reading. Of course, reading helped a great deal: it stirred, delighted, and tormented me. But at times I'd get terribly tired of it. I longed to move about, and would suddenly plunge into dark, surreptitious, sordid debauchery—not even debauchery: mean, paltry dissipation. My wretched little lusts were sharp and smarting due to my constant state of morbid irritability. I was given to hysterical outbursts, with tears and convulsions. Aside from reading, I had nothing to turn to, nothing I could then respect in my surroundings, nothing that could attract me. I would be overwhelmed with pent-up misery. I would hysterically long for contradictions, contrasts, and so I'd take to dissipation. It wasn't to justify myself that I've been telling you all this, not in the least.... Yet, no! That was precisely what I tried to do—to justify myself. I am making this little note for myself, gentlemen. I do not want to lie. I've given my word.

I gave myself up to dissipation alone, at night—secretly, furtively, sordidly, with shame that would not leave me at the most loathsome moments, that even brought me at these moments to the point of cursing. Already at that time I carried the underground in my soul. I was terrified of being seen, of meeting someone I knew, of being recognized. And I frequented all sorts of dismal haunts.

Once, passing a cheap tavern, I saw through the lighted window some gentlemen fighting with billiard cues, and one of them was thrown out of the window. At another time I might have felt revulsion, but at that moment I was suddenly overcome with envy of the man who had been thrown out, an envy so acute that I even stepped into the tavern, into the billiard room: Perhaps I too could get into a fight, and also get tossed out of the window.

I wasn't drunk—yet there you have it!—that's what misery can drive a man to. But it came to nothing. It turned out that I wasn't even capable of jumping out of the window, and I left without a fight.

I was put in my place at the very outset by a certain officer.

I stood near the billiard table, unwittingly barring the way, and he had to pass. He took me by the shoulders and silently—without warning and without apology—moved me from where I stood to another spot, and then walked by as though he had never noticed me. I could have forgiven blows, but how could I forgive just being moved like that and being so completely ignored?

The devil knows what I wouldn't have given at that moment for a proper, regular quarrel, a more decent, more *literary* one, as it were! I had been treated as if I were a fly. This officer was a six-footer, and I was undersized and puny. Nevertheless, the quarrel was up to me: I merely had to protest, and they surely would have thrown me out of the window. But I changed my mind and chose to . . . slink out, fuming with bitterness.

I left the tavern and returned home, confused and overwrought. And on the following night I went on with my little dissipations still more timidly, more furtively and sadly than before—as though with tears in my eyes. Yet I went on. But don't think I retreated before the officer out of cowardice: I have never been a coward at heart, although I was forever fearful of action. But wait before you laugh—there is an explanation for it. Rest assured, I have explanations for everything.

Ah, if this officer were one of those who'd fight a duel!

But no, he was precisely one of those gentry (long vanished, alas!) who preferred to act with billiard cues or, like Gogol's Lieutenant Pirogov,[18] to lodge complaints with the authorities. But they would not duel; and with a mere civilian penpusher like me, at any rate, they would consider dueling beneath their dignity. Besides, they generally regarded duels as something unthinkable, atheistic, French, although they were quite free with dealing out insults, especially when they were six feet tall.

I slunk out not because of cowardice, but because of boundless vanity. What frightened me was not the officer's height, or the painful thrashing I might get, or the threat of being tossed out of the window. I'm sure I would have had sufficient physical courage, but I lacked moral courage. I was afraid that everybody present—from the insolent marker down to the moldy, pimply little clerk with a greasy collar who hung about there—would misunderstand and jeer at me if I protested and spoke to them in literary Russian. Because it's still impossible in our country to speak about a point of honor—I mean, not honor itself, but a point of honor (*point d'honneur*)—otherwise than in literary language. "Points of honor" don't exist in ordinary, everyday speech.

I was absolutely certain (my sense of reality, despite all my romanticism) that all of them would simply split their sides with laughter and that the officer, instead of giving me a simple, hence inoffensive, thrashing, would be sure to kick me with his knee, driving me in this manner around the billiard table, before he might at last take mercy on me and throw me out the window.

Naturally, for me this wretched business could not end just there and then. Afterwards I often met that officer in the street and took careful note of him. But I don't know whether he recognized me. Probably not. I concluded that from certain indications. But I—I stared at him with malice and hate, and this went on . . . for several years! In fact, my hate grew with the years. First I quietly began to gather information about that officer. This was difficult, for I knew no one. But once somebody called him by name in the street when I was following him at a distance as though tied to him, and so I learned his name. Another time I trailed him all the way home, and for ten kopeks found out from the porter what floor he lived on, whether he lived alone or with someone else, and so on—in short, everything that can be learned from a porter. One morning it suddenly occurred to me, although I had never engaged in literary endeavors, to describe that officer in a kind of exposé or caricature, in the form of a story. I wrote the story with delectation. I exposed him, I even maligned him a bit. At first I gave him a name that would be immediately recognizable; later, on mature consideration, I changed it and sent the story to the *Fatherland Notes*.[19] But at that time satirical exposés were not yet in fashion, and my story was not published. I was extremely bitter about it.

There were times when I would simply suffocate with anger. At last I decided to challenge my enemy to a duel. I composed an excellent, charming letter to him, pleading with him to apologize to me, and strongly hinting at a duel in the event of his refusal. The letter was written in such a way that, if the officer had but the slightest sense of "the lofty and the beautiful," he would be sure to hasten to me and throw his arms around my neck and offer me his friendship. And how splendid that would have been! How well we could have gotten on! How beautifully we could have lived! "He would protect me with his rank and stature, and I would ennoble him with my culture and, well...ideas. And who can tell what else could come of it!"

Imagine, it was already two years since he had insulted me, and my challenge was a most preposterous anachronism despite all the cleverness of my letter, explaining and disguising the anachronism. But thank God (I still thank the Almighty with tears in my eyes), I never sent that letter. It gives me chills to think of what might have happened if I had. And suddenly . . . suddenly I avenged myself in the simplest manner—by a stroke of genius! A most brilliant idea suddenly dawned upon me. On holidays I sometimes took a stroll at four o'clock along Nevsky Prospect, usually on the sunny side. Well, actually, I was not simply strolling at all, but enduring endless torments, humiliations, and outbursts of bitter gall; yet this was evidently what I needed. I slipped in and out among the promenading crowd in a most unbecoming fashion, continually stepping out of the way of generals, cavalry officers, hussars, ladies. At those moments I suffered painful spasms in my heart, and my whole back would get hot at the mere thought of the poverty of my clothes, the wretchedness and meanness of my darting little figure. It was sheer torture, a continuous intolerable sense of humiliation at the idea, which turned into a constant and direct feeling, that I was nothing but a fly before all that fine society, a revolting, obscene fly—more intelligent, more cultivated, nobler than anyone else, that went without saying, but a fly nonetheless, forever yielding the way to everyone, humiliated and insulted by everyone. Why did I take this martyrdom upon myself? Why did I go to Nevsky? I have no idea. But I was simply *drawn* there at every opportunity.

I was already then beginning to experience that welling up of pleasure which I described in the first chapter. And after the affair with the officer, I was drawn there even more irresistibly. It was on Nevsky that I met him, it was there that I could admire him to the full. He also came there mostly on holidays. He also stepped out of the way of generals and personages of rank, and also ducked in and out among them; but men of my ilk, and even those a rung or two above, he simply crushed; he walked right at them, as if there were but empty space before him, and never yielded the way. I luxuriated in hatred watching him, and . . . each time, raging inwardly, would step aside before him. It tormented me that even in the street I couldn't manage to treat him as an equal. "Why must you step aside first?" I'd rant at myself in wild hysterics, waking up sometimes at three in the morning. "Why just you, why not he? There is, after all, no law about it, it isn't written anywhere. Why can't it be on equal terms, as always when well-bred people meet: he'll yield half, and you'll yield half, and you will pass each other with mutual respect?"

But this never happened, and I continued to step aside, while he didn't even notice that I was yielding him the right of way. And suddenly a most amazing idea dawned on me. "What," I asked myself, "if I meet him and . . . don't step aside? Just deliberately don't step aside, even if it means jostling him? What then?" This audacious idea gradually took such hold of me that it gave me no rest. I dreamed of it continually, obsessively, and purposely went to Nevsky Prospect still more often in order to picture to myself even more clearly how I would do this when I did it. I was in ecstasy. The plan seemed ever more possible and realizable to me. Of course, I wouldn't really jostle him, I thought, already relenting a little with the joy of it. I'll simply not step aside and collide with him—not very violently, but only so, shoulder against shoulder, just within the limits of propriety; so that I'll bump him exactly as hard as he bumps me.

And finally I made up my mind about it. However, preparations took a great deal of time. The first thing was to look as decent as possible during the execution of my plan, and so I had to take care of my clothes. "Just in case; if, for example, there should be a public scandal (and the public there was *superflu*:[20] a countess, Prince D., the whole literary world). I must be well dressed; this makes an impression, and will immediately place us, in a manner of speaking, on an equal footing in the eyes of high society." With this in mind, I managed to secure an advance against my salary and bought black gloves and a decent hat at Churkin's. Black gloves seemed to me more dignified and *bon ton* than the lemon-colored ones I had considered at first. "The color is too garish, too much as though one were trying to draw attention." And I did not buy the lemon-colored ones. I had already long ago prepared an excellent shirt, with white bone cuff links. The one remaining problem was my overcoat. It wasn't bad in itself, and it kept me warm; but it had a quilted lining and a raccoon collar, and this was altogether like a lackey's. It was essential at any cost to change the collar to beaver, such as officers wore. To this end I began to frequent Gostiny Dvor and, after several attempts, decided on a certain inexpensive German beaver. These German beavers wore out very fast and became wretchedly shabby, but when new they looked well—indeed, quite well. And all I needed it for was just this one occasion. I inquired about the price—it was still too high. After serious consideration, I decided to sell my raccoon collar and to ask Anton Antonych Setochkin, my office chief, to lend me the difference—for me, quite a considerable one. Anton Antonych was a modest but a serious and solid man, who never lent money to anyone. However, on first coming to the office, I had been particularly recommended to him by the eminent personage who had obtained this employment for me. I suffered dreadfully. Asking Anton Antonych for a loan seemed monstrous and shameful to me. In fact, I could not sleep for two or three nights; but I generally slept poorly at that time. I was in a fever. My heart would sink, as if about to stop, then suddenly begin to thump and thump!

At first Anton Antonych was surprised, then he frowned, then thought it over and did give me the loan, making me sign a note authorizing him to deduct the borrowed sum two weeks later from my salary. And so everything was finally ready. The handsome beaver was installed in place of the mangy raccoon, and I gradually began to prepare myself for action. After all, I couldn't plunge into it at once, any old way; I had to go about it skillfully, step by step. But I confess, after numerous attempts I had almost begun to despair: we did not bump into each other, no matter what! For all my preparations, for all my firm resolve—and time and time again it seemed that just another moment, and we would collide, yet no—I'd step aside again, and he would pass by without noticing me. I even prayed as I approached him, I begged God to inspire me with determination. One day I was fully set to do it, but all that happened was that I stumbled underfoot, because at the very last moment, just two inches away from him, I lost courage. He very calmly stepped across me, and I bounced aside like a rubber ball. That night I was sick again, feverish and delirious. Then suddenly everything came to the best possible conclusion.

On the eve of that day I had made a final decision to abandon my ruinous plan and to dismiss it all. With that in mind, I went to Nevsky for the last time, simply to see how I would dismiss it all. And suddenly, three steps away from my enemy, I made up my mind in an instant, shut my eyes, and—we collided firmly, shoulder against shoulder! I did not yield an inch and passed him by entirely on an equal footing! He did not even glance back and pretended he hadn't noticed anything; but he was only pretending, I am convinced of that! I am convinced of it to this day. Naturally, I got the worst of the collision, for he was stronger, but that was not the point. The point was that I had achieved my goal, I had sustained my dignity, I had not yielded a step and had publicly set myself on an equal social footing with him. I came home fully avenged for everything. I was jubilant. I was ecstatic and sang Italian arias. Naturally, I will not describe to you what happened to me three days later; if you have read my first chapter, "Underground," you may surmise it yourself. The officer was later transferred somewhere; I have not seen him for some fourteen years. How is he doing nowadays, the good man? Whom is he crushing now?

II

BUT AS the phase of dissipation would draw to an end, a dreadful nausea would come over me. I was tormented by remorse, and I would try to drive it away: it was all too sickening. Little by little, however, I would get used to this too. I would get used to everything, or perhaps, not so much get used to it as somehow consent to endure it. But I had a way out, which reconciled everything: escape into "the lofty and the beautiful"—in my dreams, of course. I was a terrible dreamer; I would dream for three months on end, huddled in my corner. And, I assure you, at those times I was entirely unlike the gentleman who had sewn the German beaver collar to his coat in chicken-hearted anxiety. I'd suddenly become a heroic figure. I wouldn't even have allowed the six-foot lieutenant to cross my threshold, had he come to visit me. I couldn't even have imagined him before me.

What were my dreams, and how did I manage to content myself with them? I cannot tell you now, but at that time I did find satisfaction in them. Although, of course, I satisfy myself with dreams to some extent today as well. These dreams were all the sweeter and keener after my little debauches; they came amidst penitence and tears, curses and exaltations. There were moments of such absolute rapture, such happiness, that I did not feel the slightest trace of mockery within me—I swear I didn't. There were only faith, hope, and love. And that is just the point: at those moments I had a blind belief that, by some miracle, through some external circumstance, everything would suddenly expand, enlarge itself; that a broad horizon of appropriate activity—beneficent, sublime, and, best of all, *entirely ready* to be entered on—would open up before me (I never knew what this activity would be, but the most important thing about it was that it would be entirely ready). And I would suddenly come forth into God's world, all but riding a white steed and crowned with laurel.

I could not conceive of a secondary role, and this was precisely why in reality I very calmly occupied the lowest. Either a hero, or mud; there was no middle. Indeed, this is what ruined me, because, mired down in filth, I would console myself with the thought that at other times I was a hero, and the hero redeemed the filth. As if to say: it would be shameful for an ordinary man to get mired down, but a hero is too sublime to be completely defiled, hence he could wallow in filth.

It is remarkable that these surges of "the lofty and the beautiful" would come upon me during my little bouts of dissipation as well, and just when I was at the very lowest depths. They came in spurts, as though to remind me of themselves. Nevertheless, they did not end the dissipation by their appearance; on the contrary, they seemed to give it added zest by contrast, and came precisely in sufficient proportion to lend it proper seasoning. This seasoning consisted of contradictions and suffering, of agonizing inner analysis, and all the pinpricks and torments lent my slimy little dissipations a certain piquancy, and even significance. In short, it performed the function of a good sauce. And all of this might even be said to have contained a certain depth of meaning. For would I ever have consented to the simple, vulgar little debauchery of an ordinary clerk, and endured the filth of it? How could it have succeeded, then, in enticing me and luring me into the street at night? No, sir, I had a noble loophole ready for every possible occasion....

Yet how much love, Lord, how much love I experienced in those dreams of mine, in those "escapes into everything lofty and beautiful." This love might have existed only in fantasy, it might never have been applied to any human situation in reality, but it was so abundant, so overflowing, that afterwards there wasn't even any need to apply it in practice; that would have been too much of a luxury. Everything, however, always ended most satisfactorily— in a lazy and ecstatic transition to the realm of art; that is, to beautiful modes of existence, entirely ready-made, largely stolen from poets and novelists and adapted to serve every need and demand.

For example: I would triumph over everybody; naturally, they would all be prostrate in the dust and compelled to voluntarily acknowledge my perfections, while I forgave them all. Or else I was a famous poet and court chamberlain, and fell in love. I received countless millions and immediately gave them away for the benefit of humanity, at the same moment confessing before the crowd all my infamies, which, of course, were not mere infamies, but also contained within them a wealth of "the lofty and the beautiful," of something Manfred-like.[21] Everyone would weep and kiss me (naturally, or they'd be impossible dolts), and I would go off, barefoot and hungry, to preach new ideas and to rout the reactionaries at Austerlitz. Then a march would strike up, an amnesty would be granted, and the Pope would agree to move from Rome to Brazil; then a ball would be given for the whole of Italy at the Villa Borghese, situated on the shore of Lake Como, since Lake Como would have been brought for this occasion to Rome. Then there would be a scene in the shrubbery, and so on, and so forth—don't you know it all?

You will say that it is cheap and banal to bring all this into the open, after so many raptures and tears, to which I myself have admitted. But why cheap? Do you really think I am ashamed of it, or that it was sillier than anything in your own lives? Besides, believe me, gentlemen, some of it was rather nicely composed. . . . After all, not everything took place on the shore of Lake Como. However, you are right; it's really cheap and banal. And the worst of it is that I have begun to justify myself before you. And even worse, that I am making this remark now. But enough, or there will be no end to it: whatever I say or do will be cheaper and nastier than what has gone before. . . .

I was never able to dream consistently for more than three months, after which I would develop an irresistible urge to plunge into society. Plunging into society meant in my case visiting my office chief, Anton Antonych Setochkin. He was the only lasting acquaintance I've had in my lifetime; in fact, I wonder at it now myself. But even to him I would go only when my dream phase reached such a degree of happiness that I would feel an overwhelming need to embrace all people, all mankind, immediately, at once. And that required the presence of at least one person existing in reality. Anton Antonych could be visited, however, only on Tuesdays (his "at home" days); hence it was always necessary to time my need to embrace mankind to Tuesdays.

This Anton Antonych lived at Five Corners, on the fourth floor, in four low-ceilinged rooms, each smaller than the last, and all of them yellowish and most frugal in appearance. He lived with two daughters and their aunt, who would serve tea. The daughters—one was thirteen, the other fourteen—were both snub-nosed, and I was terribly shy with them because they kept whispering to each other and giggling. The host usually sat in his study on a leather sofa in front of his desk, together with some gray-haired guest, an official from our department, or even from some other. I never met more than two or three guests there, always the same ones. They talked about excise duties, debates in the Senate, salaries, promotions, His Excellency and ways of pleasing him, and so on. I had the patience to sit like a fool with those people, listening to them for four hours on end, and never daring to say a word or knowing what to say. I would fall into a stupor and break out in perspiration again and again. Paralysis hung over me. But it was good and beneficial. When I returned home, I would put away my longing to embrace all of humanity for a while.

I had, however, yet another acquaintance of sorts—a former schoolmate, Simonov. In fact, I had many old schoolfellows in Petersburg, but I did not associate with them and had stopped greeting them in the street. Perhaps I had even gone to work in another department in order not to be with them, to cut myself off once for all from my whole detestable childhood. Damn that school, damn those dreadful years of penal servitude! In short, as soon as I was free, I immediately broke with my schoolmates. There were only two or three whom I still greeted on meeting. One of these was Simonov, who had not distinguished himself in any way at school. He was quiet and even-tempered, but I discerned in him a certain independence of character and even honesty. I don't even think he was so very mediocre. We had had some rather bright moments together once upon a time, but they did not last; somehow they clouded over suddenly. He evidently found these recollections irksome and, I think, feared that I might fall back into the former tone. I suspected that he felt extreme aversion to me, yet I continued to visit him, not quite certain that it was so.

Well, one Thursday, unable to endure my solitude any longer and knowing that Anton Antonych's doors were shut on Thursdays, I thought of Simonov. As I climbed to his fourth-floor apartment, I was thinking that this gentleman found my presence irksome and that I should not be going there. But since such thoughts would always in the end goad me still more irresistibly, as though in spite, into dubious situations, I went in. It was almost a year since I had last seen Simonov.

III

I FOUND two other former schoolmates with him. They seemed to be discussing an important matter and paid scarcely any attention to my coming—which, in fact, was rather odd, since I had not seen them for many years. They obviously regarded me as no more than an ordinary fly. I had not been subjected to such slights even at school, though everybody hated me there. I understood, of course, that they were bound to despise me now for my lack of success in the service, for letting myself go to seed so badly, for my shabby clothes, and so on, which in their eyes were proof of my ineptness and insignificance. Nevertheless, I was not prepared for such a degree of contempt. Simonov even appeared surprised to see me. But then, my visits always seemed to surprise him. Disconcerted by all this, I sat down somewhat dejectedly and began to listen to their conversation.

They were discussing earnestly, even excitedly, a farewell dinner which these gentlemen wished to arrange on the following day for their friend Zverkov, an officer, who was leaving for a distant province. Monsieur Zverkov had been my schoolmate too. I began to hate him particularly in the higher grades. In the lower grades he had been merely a pretty, high-spirited boy whom everybody liked. However, I detested him in the lower grades as well, precisely because he was a pretty and high-spirited boy. He was always a poor student, getting worse as time went on; nevertheless, he graduated successfully because he had influential connections. During his last year at school he inherited an estate of two hundred serfs, and since most of us were poor, he took to strutting and swaggering before us. He was an extremely vulgar fellow, though good-hearted even when he strutted. But despite the fantastic, high-flown, purely external notions of pride and honor among us, almost everybody, with few exceptions, fawned upon Zverkov, and the more so the more he strutted. And it was not for the sake of any advantage that they fawned on him, but simply because he was a man favored by the gifts of nature.

Moreover, Zverkov was regarded among us as an authority on social graces and good manners. This latter especially infuriated me. I hated his sharp, self-confident tone of voice, his admiration for his own witticisms, which were terribly flat despite his bold tongue; I hated his handsome but foolish face (for which I nevertheless would gladly have traded my *intelligent* one) and his free and easy bearing, in fashion among officers during the 'forties. I hated his boasting of his future amorous conquests (he did not venture to take up with women before receiving his officer's epaulettes and looked forward to them impatiently) and of the innumerable duels he was going to fight. I remember how, despite my usual silence, I suddenly lashed into him one day during recess when I heard him bragging to his comrades about his future exploits and finally, carried away by his excitement like a puppy in the sun, declaring that he wouldn't leave a single village girl on his estate without his attentions. This was his *droit de seigneur*. And if the peasants dared to protest, he would have them all flogged and double their tax, the bearded rascals that they were.

Our louts applauded him, and I attacked him, not at all out of sympathy for the virgins and their fathers, but simply because such a nonentity got such applause. I got the best of him, but Zverkov, though stupid, was gay and impudent and therefore laughed it off, so that, in fact, I hadn't altogether gotten the best of him; the laugh remained on his side. Afterwards he got the best of me on several other occasions, without malice, but somehow in jest, in passing, with a laugh. I kept a spiteful and contemptuous silence, and would not answer him. After graduation he made an effort to become friendlier; I was not too unreceptive, because it flattered me. But we quickly and naturally drifted apart. Later I heard about his barrack-room successes as a lieutenant and the *wild life* he was leading. Still later there were other rumors, about his *advances* in the service. He no longer greeted me in the street, and I suspected that he was afraid to compromise himself by greeting so insignificant a person as myself. I also saw him once at the theater, in a box, already wearing shoulder knots. He was bowing and scraping before the daughters of some ancient general. He had let himself go rather badly in the three years since he had left school, though he was still quite handsome and graceful; he somehow sagged and had begun to put on weight. It was obvious that by the age of thirty he would be altogether fat and flabby. It was for this Zverkov, who was leaving town, that our former schoolfellows wanted to arrange a dinner. They had kept up relations with him throughout those three years, though inwardly, I'm sure, they did not consider themselves his equals.

One of Simonov's visitors was Ferfichkin, a Russified German—a short, monkey-faced fool who always mocked and mimicked everybody. He was my bitterest enemy from the earliest grades, a nasty, insolent little braggart who affected the touchiest sense of honor, though, naturally, he was nothing but a petty coward at heart. He was one of Zverkov's admirers who truckled to him for ulterior motives and often borrowed money from him. The other visitor, Trudolyubov, was an entirely unremarkable individual, a military fellow, tall, with a cold expression, fairly honest but a worshiper of all success and capable of discussing only one topic—promotions. He was a distant relation of Zverkov's and this, silly to say, lent him a certain standing among us. He had always regarded me as a nobody, but though his treatment of me was not altogether polite, it was tolerable.

"Well," said Trudolyubov, "at seven rubles each— twenty-one for the three of us—we can have a good dinner. Zverkov, of course, doesn't pay."

"Naturally, since we're inviting him," decided Simonov.

"Do you really think," Ferfichkin broke in heatedly, like an insolent lackey bragging of his master's medals, "do you really think Zverkov will let us pay it all? He will accept out of delicacy, but he's sure to order half a dozen bottles as his share."

"Half a dozen, for just the four of us?" said Trudolyubov, taking notice only of the half-dozen.

"Well, then. It's the three of us, with Zverkov the fourth, twenty-one rubles, at the Hôtel de Paris, tomorrow at five." Simonov, who had been chosen to make the arrangements, concluded the discussion.

"But why twenty-one?" I asked with some agitation, perhaps even with resentment. "Counting me, it will be twenty-eight rubles, not twenty-one."

It seemed to me that this sudden and unexpected offer to join in would be a handsome gesture; it would immediately win them over and raise me in their estimation.

"Oh, you wish to come too?" Simonov asked with displeasure, somehow trying to avoid my eyes. He knew me through and through.

It infuriated me that he knew me through and through.

"But why? I'd think I'm also an old schoolmate, and, frankly, I resent being left out." I began to boil over again.

"And where were we supposed to look for you?" Ferfichkin broke in rudely.

"You were never on good terms with Zverkov," Trudolyubov added, frowning. But I had already fastened on to the idea and wouldn't let go.

"It seems to me that no one has a right to judge that," I

argued in a trembling voice, as though God knows what were happening. "Perhaps that's why I want to come now, precisely because we were not on good terms."

"Oh, well, who could ever make you out... all those high-flown notions..." said Trudolyubov with a dry grin.

"We'll put your name down," Simonov decided, turning to me. "Tomorrow at five, at the Hôtel de Paris; you'll remember."

"And what about the money?" Ferfichkin said in an undertone to Simonov, nodding at me, but he broke off, because even Simonov was embarrassed.

"That will do," Trudolyubov said, getting up. "If he's so eager, let him come."

"But this is our own intimate circle," Ferfichkin grumbled, also picking up his hat. "It isn't an official gathering. Perhaps we do not want your company at all...."

They left. Ferfichkin did not even trouble to say goodbye to me. Trudolyubov barely nodded, without looking. Simonov, with whom I remained alone, was in a state of baffled irritation and gave me a strange look. He did not sit down and did not invite me to.

"Hm... well... tomorrow, then. Do you want to give me the money now? I mean, just to be sure," he muttered in confusion.

I flushed, but as I flushed I suddenly recalled the fifteen rubles I had owed Simonov for heaven knew how long, which, in truth, I had never forgotten, but never paid either.

"You must realize, Simonov, that I couldn't possibly have known when I came... and I'm dreadfully sorry I forgot...."

"Oh, well, oh, well, it doesn't matter. You will pay tomorrow at dinnertime. I merely wanted to know.... Please, don't...."

He broke off and started pacing the room with even greater irritation. As he paced, he began to bear down on his heels, stamping more and more loudly.

"I am not detaining you?" I asked after two minutes of silence.

"Oh, no!" he suddenly recalled himself. "I mean, actually—yes. You see, I must still drop over.... It's not too far from here..." he added in an oddly apologetic voice, with some embarrassment.

"Oh, heavens! Why didn't you say so!" I exclaimed, snatching up my hat—but with an astonishingly free and easy air that came upon me suddenly from God knows where.

"It really isn't far.... Just a few steps away..." Simonov kept repeating as he saw me to the door with a fluttery air that did not in the least become him. "Tomorrow at five, then, punctually!" he called down after me—he was so pleased at my leaving. But I was in a rage.

"The devil! What the devil got into me!" I gnashed my teeth, striding down the street. "And for that scoundrel, that pig Zverkov! Of course, I mustn't go. Of course. To hell with them. I'm not bound to them, am I? I'll let Simonov know tomorrow by mail...."

But I was in a rage precisely because I knew beyond all doubt that I would go, that I would go just out of spite. And the more tactless, the more improper my going, the more sure I was to go.

In fact, there was even a definite obstacle to my going: I had no money. All I had was nine rubles, but out of that seven had to be paid the very next day to my servant, Apollon—his monthly wage, with board at his own expense.

And it was impossible not to pay him, considering Apollon's character. But more about this rascal, this bane of my existence, some other time.

Nevertheless, I knew that I would not pay him, after all, and would make sure to go.

That night I had the most revolting dreams, and no

wonder: all evening I was oppressed by recollections about the penal servitude of my school years, and could not rid myself of them. I had been shunted off into that school by distant relatives whose dependent I was and of whom I have never heard since. They left me there, a lonely boy, already crushed by their reproaches, already brooding, silent, looking at everything with savage suspicion. My schoolmates met me with vicious and merciless ridicule because I was unlike any of them. But I could not endure ridicule; and I could not get along with others as easily as they did. I conceived an immediate hatred for them and shut myself away from everyone in timid, wounded, and inordinate pride. Their rudeness revolted me. They cynically mocked my face and my awkward figure; yet how stupid their own faces were! In our school facial expressions somehow degenerated and lapsed into particular stupidity. So many charming boys came to the school, yet after a few years they would be sickening to look at. Already at the age of sixteen I wondered at them gloomily; I was amazed at the pettiness of their minds, the stupidity of their activities, games, and conversations. They were so lacking in understanding of the most essential things, so devoid of interest in the most important, most remarkable matters, that I involuntarily began to look upon them as my inferiors. It wasn't wounded vanity that led me to this, and for God's sake, don't come to me with the nauseatingly stale cliché that "I was only dreaming, while they understood life's realities already at that age." They understood nothing, none of life's realities, and, I swear to you, this was what made me most indignant. Quite the contrary. They responded to the most obvious, glaring realities with fantastic obtuseness, and already then worshiped nothing but success.

With heartless and shameful cruelty they mocked all that was just, but crushed and humbled. They mistook rank for intelligence; at sixteen they were already talking of finding a soft berth. Naturally, much of this was due to stupidity, to the bad examples that surrounded them in their childhood and boyhood. They were monstrously depraved. Of course, this too was mostly superficial, an affectation of cynicism; of course, there were still glints of youth and some degree of freshness even beneath their depravity. But even this freshness lacked charm and expressed itself in a sort of rakish swagger.

I hated them dreadfully, although I was, perhaps, still worse than they. They paid me back in kind and did not trouble to conceal their loathing. But I no longer wanted their affection; on the contrary, I constantly longed to see them humiliated. To rid myself of their taunts, I applied myself to my studies and became one of the best students. This impressed them. Besides, they all gradually began to realize that I had already read books that were far beyond them and understood things (not included in our special courses) which they had not even heard of. They regarded this with astonished mockery, but morally they yielded to it, especially since even the teachers began to notice me in this connection. The taunts ceased, but hostility remained, and our relations were cold and strained.

In the end I myself could bear it no longer: with the years, the need for people, for friends increased. I made some attempts to form closer ties with certain boys, but the relationships always turned out to be awkward and unnatural and somehow dissolved of themselves. Once I even had a friend. But I was already a despot at heart; I wanted to wield unlimited power over his soul; I sought to instill in him contempt for his surroundings; I demanded his complete and disdainful break with these surroundings. I frightened him off with my passionate friendship; I'd reduce him to tears, to convulsions. He was a naive and devoted soul; but when he submitted himself to me completely, I immediately began to detest him and repulsed him—as if all I had needed him for was merely to conquer, to subjugate him. But I could not subjugate everybody; my friend was also unlike any of the others, a rare exception. My first step on graduating from school was to leave the special department I had been trained for in order to break all ties, to curse the past and cover it with dust. . . . And the devil knows why, after all that, I dragged myself to this Simonov! . . .

In the morning I roused myself early and leaped out of bed, as excited as if everything was to start happening at once. I felt I was on the verge of a radical change in my life, and that this change would come that very day. Perhaps it was because I was so unaccustomed to external events, but always, whenever anything, no matter how trivial, occurred, it seemed to me that some radical turn in my life was just about to take place. Nevertheless, I went to work as usual, but slipped away two hours earlier in order to prepare myself. The main thing, I felt, was not to be the first to come, or they would think that I was much too overjoyed at the occasion. But there were thousands of such "main things," and they all agitated me to the point of exhaustion.

With my own hands I polished my boots a second time; Apollon would never in the world have polished them twice on the same day, considering that to be improper. And so I polished them with the brushes I had stolen from the foyer, making sure he wouldn't notice and begin to despise me afterwards. Then I made a careful examination of my clothes and found that everything was old, shabby, bedraggled. I had let myself become too slovenly. My office uniform was more or less in order, but I couldn't, after all, go to dinner in my uniform. And worst of all, on my trousers, right on the knee, there was a huge yellowish spot. I knew in advance that this spot alone would rob me of nine-tenths of my self-respect. I also knew that it was mean to think so. "But this is no time for thinking; now I am facing reality," I kept saying to myself and losing courage. I also knew perfectly well that I was wildly exaggerating the importance of all these facts. But what could I do? I was no longer able to control myself; I shook as in a fever. Despairingly, I imagined how that "swine" Zverkov would meet me with cold disdain; how that dunce Trudolyubov would look at me with dull, unshakable contempt; how nastily and impudently that vermin Ferfichkin would giggle at my expense, playing up to Zverkov; how perfectly Simonov would understand all this, and how he would despise me in his heart for the meanness of my vanity and cowardice. And, worst of all, how paltry, how *unliterary,* how ordinary it would all be.

Of course, it would be best not to go at all. But that was altogether impossible: once I was drawn to anything, I'd plunge in all the way, over my head. I would have jeered at myself for it afterwards to the end of my days: "So you've backed out, eh? You've backed out before *reality!* You've backed out!" No, I passionately longed to prove to all that "trash" that I was in no way the coward I imagined myself to be. But that wasn't all: in the most violent paroxysm of cowardly fever, I dreamed of winning the upper hand, of conquering, of carrying them away, of forcing them to love me—if only for my "nobility of mind and unquestionable wit." They would abandon Zverkov, he would sit at the side, silent and shamed, and I would crush him. Afterwards I would perhaps make peace with him and drink to our *friendship.* But the most cruel and humiliating thing to me was that I knew even then, surely and completely, that I really needed none of this at all; that, in truth, I had no desire whatever to crush them, or win them over, or attract them; and that, even had I achieved this, I'd be the first to say it wasn't worth a straw. But oh, how I prayed to God for the day to be over! With inexpressible anguish I kept going to the window, opening the transom, and peering into the grayish murk of densely falling wet snow. . . .

At last my broken-down old wall clock wheezed out

the hour of five. I snatched up my hat, and trying not to
look at Apollon—who had been waiting for his wage
since morning, but wouldn't speak first out of pride—I
slipped past him out of the door and, for my last half ru-
ble, hired a coachman, just to drive up to the Hôtel de
Paris like a lord.

IV

I KNEW in advance that I would be the first. But now it
was no longer a question of who was first.

Not only were none of them there, but I had difficulty in
finding our room. The table had not yet been set. What
could it mean? After numerous inquiries I finally learned
from the waiters that the dinner had been ordered for six
o'clock instead of five. This was confirmed at the buffet.
By that time I was already ashamed of asking. It was still
only twenty after five. If they had changed the hour, they
should at any rate have notified me—that was what the city
post office was for—and not subject me to "disgrace" both
before myself and... well, even before the servants. I sat
down. A waiter began to set the table; in his presence I felt
even more humiliated. By six, candles were brought into
the room, in addition to the lighted lamps. The waiter had
not thought, however, of bringing them as soon as I arrived. In the next room two gloomy guests, angry-looking
and silent, were dining at separate tables. From one of the
distant rooms came a good deal of noise; I could hear
shouting and the uproarious laughter of a crowd of people
and odious little squeals and exclamations in French: there
were ladies at that dinner. In short, it was extremely de-
pressing. I had rarely spent a more wretched hour, so that

when they appeared, all together, exactly at six, I was even, for a moment, overjoyed to see them, as though they were some sort of liberators, almost forgetting that I must look offended.

Zverkov entered first, the obvious leader. Both he and they were laughing. But, seeing me, Zverkov drew himself up, approached me unhurriedly, bowing slightly, almost coquettishly, at the waist, and offered me his hand, amiably enough though not overly so, with a certain careful civility, for all the world like a general, as if, offering his hand, he was also guarding himself against something. I had imagined, on the contrary, that as soon as he came in, he would break into his old, high-pitched laughter, punctuated with little squeals, and would immediately launch into his flat jokes and witticisms. This was what I had tried to prepare myself for ever since the previous evening, but I had never expected such condescension, such general-like benevolence. So he was now entirely convinced of his immeasurable superiority over me in all respects! If he merely intended to insult me by that condescending manner, I thought, it wouldn't be so bad; I'd manage to retaliate somehow. But what if, without meaning to insult me, he had really taken it into his stupid sheep's brain that he was immeasurably superior to me and could no longer regard me in any way but patronizingly? The very possibility made me gasp for air.

"I was astonished to learn of your desire to join us," he began, simpering and lisping and stretching out his words, which he had never done in the past. "We've somehow gotten out of contact. You avoid us. A pity. We aren't as dreadful as you think. Well, sir, at any rate I am pleased to renew..."

And he turned carelessly to put his hat down on the windowsill.

"Have you been waiting long?" asked Trudolyubov.

"I came exactly at five, as I was informed yesterday," I

answered loudly and with irritation that promised an imminent explosion.

"Didn't you let him know the hour had been changed?" Trudolyubov turned to Simonov.

"I didn't. I forgot," he answered without any sign of regret, and, not troubling to apologize, he went out to arrange for the hors d'oeuvres.

"So you've been waiting an hour, you poor fellow!" Zverkov exclaimed mockingly, for, according to his lights, this must indeed have seemed extremely funny. The scoundrel Ferfichkin echoed him in a high, vile little titter, like the yipping of a nasty pup. He also thought my situation terribly funny and embarrassing.

"It's not the least bit amusing!" I cried to Ferfichkin, becoming more and more irritated. "It's someone else's fault, not mine. No one took the trouble to let me know. It's—it's—it's.... simply preposterous."

"Not only preposterous, but something else as well," grumbled Trudolyubov, naively taking my side. "You are much too indulgent. It's plain rudeness. Unintentional, of course. How could Simonov... hm!"

"If anyone played such a trick on me," remarked Ferfichkin, "I'd..."

"Oh, you'd have ordered something," Zverkov interrupted, "or simply asked for your dinner without waiting."

"You must allow that I could have done so without anyone's permission," I snapped. "If I waited, that means..."

"Be seated, gentlemen," cried Simonov, entering. "Everything is ready. I can vouch for the champagne, it's excellently chilled.... I didn't know your address," he suddenly turned to me. "How was I to find you?" But again he avoided my eyes. It was clear he had something against me. He must have thought things over since yesterday.

Everyone sat down. I did too. The table was round. On my left was Trudolyubov, on the right Simonov. Zverkov sat down across from me, Ferfichkin next to him, between him and Trudolyubov.

"If I may ask, are you...in a government de-part-ment?" Zverkov continued to center his attention on me. Seeing me embarrassed, he had seriously decided that I needed befriending and, so to speak, encouragement. "Does he want to make me throw a bottle at him?" I raged within myself. Unaccustomed as I was to company, I was somehow unnaturally quick to take offense.

"At the...office," I replied gruffly, staring into the plate.

"And...do you f-find it a-advantageous? T-tell me, wha-at made you leave your for-mer po-sition?"

"Wha-at made me leave my fo-ormer position was that I wanted to leave it." I stretched out my words three times as much as he did, almost beside myself now. Ferfichkin snorted. Simonov gave me an ironic look. Trudolyubov stopped eating and began to study me with curiosity.

Zverkov was irked, but he refused to take notice.

"A-a-ah, and how about your maintenance?"

"What maintenance?"

"I mean, s-salary."

"What's all this interrogation?"

Nevertheless, I immediately told him what my salary was. I blushed violently.

"Not much," Zverkov remarked with an air of self-importance.

"Yes, sir, you cannot dine at café-restaurants on that!" Ferfichkin added insolently.

"I think it's simply a pittance," Trudolyubov said earnestly.

"And how thin you've gotten, how you have changed...since..." added Zverkov, with a touch of venom now, and with a kind of impudent sympathy, examining me and my attire.

"Oh, stop embarrassing him," Ferfichkin cried, snickering.

"My dear sir, I'll have you know that I'm not embarrassed," I finally exploded. "Do you hear me! I am dining at this 'café-restaurant' at my own expense, not someone else's, please take note of that, *Monsieur* Ferfichkin."

"W-what do you mean? Who's dining here at someone else's expense? You seem to..." Ferfichkin seized on my words, turning red as a lobster, staring me in the eyes with fury.

"Just tha-at," I answered, feeling that I had gone too far. "And I think it might be better for us to turn to somewhat more intelligent conversation."

"You evidently intend to demonstrate your intellect?"

"Don't worry, that would be quite superfluous here."

"My dear sir, what's all this cackling, eh? You haven't lost your wits entirely, have you, in that *le*partment of yours?"

"Enough, gentlemen, enough!" cried Zverkov with a masterful air.

"How stupid!" muttered Simonov.

"Really stupid. We've come together in close company to give our good friend a send-off before his journey, and you talk of money," Trudolyubov said rudely, addressing me alone. "Last night you forced yourself upon us. Well then, stop disrupting the general harmony...."

"Enough, enough," shouted Zverkov. "Stop it, gentlemen, this won't do. Better let me tell you how I almost got married the other day...."

And he launched into a most unsavory anecdote on how he had almost gotten married the other day. There was, incidentally, not a word about marriage in the story, but it was peppered with the names of generals, colonels, and even court officials, with Zverkov playing virtually the leading role among them. The company laughed approvingly. Ferfichkin even shrieked with delight.

I sat ignored by everyone, crushed and annihilated.

Good Lord, is this fit company for me? I thought. And what a fool I've made of myself before them! But I permitted this Ferfichkin to go too far. The numbskulls think they've done me a favor by letting me sit at their table, they don't understand that it's I, I who am honoring them, and not the other way around! "How thin you've gotten! Your suit!" Damn those trousers! Zverkov noticed the yellow stain on the knee right away.... But what am I doing here? I must get up from the table at once, this very moment, and simply leave without a word.... Out of contempt! And tomorrow—anything, even a duel. The scoundrels. Should I be concerned about the seven rubles? They may think ... The devil take it! I don't care if I lose the seven rubles! I'll go, right now! ...

Of course, I stayed.

In my misery, I drank sherry and Lafitte by the glassful. Being unaccustomed to alcohol, I rapidly began to get drunk, and the more drunk, the more resentful I became. I suddenly longed to insult them in a most impudent fashion and then leave; to seize an appropriate moment and show them what I was worth: let them say—he may be ludicrous, but he is clever ... and ... and ... in a word, to hell with them!

I arrogantly turned my glazing eyes from one to the other. But they appeared to have forgotten me entirely. *They* were noisy, shouting, gay. Zverkov did most of the talking. I began to listen. He was telling about a certain elegant lady whom he had led on until she finally confessed her love for him (of course, he was lying shamelessly), and how he had been particularly aided in this affair by an intimate friend of his, some princeling, Kolya, a hussar, who owned three thousand serfs.

"But as I see, this Kolya, who owns three thousand serfs, hasn't bothered to come here to see you off," I suddenly broke into the conversation. For a second everyone fell silent.

"You are already drunk." Trudolyubov finally deigned to notice me, with a contemptuous glance in my direction. Zverkov silently stared at me as if I were a gnat. I dropped my eyes. Simonov hastened to pour another round of champagne.

Trudolyubov raised his glass, followed by everyone except me.

"Your health, and good luck on your journey!" he cried to Zverkov. "To old times, gentlemen, to our future, hurrah!"

Everyone drank and crowded around Zverkov to kiss him. I did not stir; the full glass stood untouched before me.

"Aren't you drinking?" Trudolyubov, losing patience, bellowed at me threateningly.

"I want to make my own speech.... Then I will drink, Mr. Trudolyubov."

"Nasty little bastard!" muttered Simonov.

I drew myself up in my chair and feverishly lifted my glass, preparing for something extraordinary, though I myself did not know exactly what I would say.

"Silence!" Ferfichkin cried. "Now, for a show of intelligence!"

Zverkov waited gravely, realizing what was happening.

"Mr. Lieutenant Zverkov," I began. "I want you to know that I detest phrases, phrasemongers, and pinched waists.... That is the first point, and now to the second."

Everyone stirred uneasily.

"Point number two: I hate smut, and I hate people who relish smut. Particularly the latter!

"Point number three: I love truth, sincerity, and honesty." I went on almost automatically, for I was turning cold with horror myself, unable to understand how I could say such things.... "I love ideas, Monsieur Zverkov; I love true comradeship, on an equal footing, and not...hm...I love....But, after all, why not? I'll drink to your health too, Monsieur Zverkov. Go on, seduce Circassian beauties, shoot down the enemies of our homeland, and... and... Your health, Monsieur Zverkov!"

Zverkov rose from his chair, bowed to me, and said:

"I am most grateful to you."

He was terribly offended and had even turned pale.

"The devil take it!" roared Trudolyubov, banging his fist on the table.

"No, people are punched in the jaw for such things!" squealed Ferfichkin.

"He ought to be kicked out!" muttered Simonov.

"Not a word, gentlemen, not a move!" Zverkov cried solemnly, curbing the general indignation. "I thank you all, but I'm quite capable of showing him myself how much value I attach to his words."

"Mr. Ferfichkin, tomorrow you will give me satisfaction for the words you have just spoken!" I said loudly, turning to Ferfichkin with dignity.

"You mean, a duel? At your service," he replied. But I must have looked so ridiculous challenging him, and it was so incongruous with my whole figure, that everybody, and Ferfichkin after them, simply shook with laugher.

"Of course, we must get rid of him! He's altogether drunk now!" Trudolyubov said with loathing.

"I shall never forgive myself for accepting him," Simonov muttered again.

Now's just the right moment to throw a bottle at them all, I thought, and, picking up a bottle, I... poured myself a full glass.

No, I had better stay here to the end, I went on to myself. You'd be delighted, gentlemen, to see me go. Not for the world. Just for spite, I'll go on sitting here and drinking to the very end, to show you that I do not consider you of any account at all. I'll sit and drink, because this is a tavern, and I've paid my admission price. I'll sit and drink, because I regard you as mere pawns, nonexistent pawns. I'll sit and drink...and sing, if I feel like it; yes, sir, I'll sing too, because I have a right to...to sing...hm.

But I did not sing. I merely tried not to look at any of them. I assumed the most nonchalant poses and waited impatiently for them to talk to me *first*. But alas, they didn't talk to me. And how much, how much I longed at that moment for a reconciliation with them! The clock struck eight, then finally nine. They abandoned the table for the sofa. Zverkov sprawled out on the sofa, putting one foot on a small round table. They brought the wine there, too. He had indeed ordered three bottles for them as his share. Naturally, he did not invite me to join. They gathered around him on the sofa. They listened to him almost with adoration. It was obvious that they were fond of him. "What for? What for?" I asked myself. From time to time, in drunken ecstasy, they would embrace and kiss. They talked about the Caucasus, the nature of true passion, a certain card game then in vogue, and lucrative positions in the service. They discussed the income of a certain hussar, Podkharzhevsky, whom none of them knew personally, and rejoiced because it was so large; they spoke of the extraordinary grace and beauty of a Princess D., whom none of them had ever seen; and finally they came to the conclusion that Shakespeare is immortal.

I smiled derisively and paced along the wall directly opposite the sofa, from table to stove and back.

I made every effort to show them that I could do very well without them, yet I deliberately stamped my feet, stepping hard on my heels. But all in vain. *They* paid me no attention whatsoever. I had the patience to pace like that, directly before them, from eight until eleven o'clock, back and forth along the same wall, from table to stove, from stove to table. "I'm just strolling here, and no one can forbid me." The waiter who entered the room now and then stopped several times to stare at me; I was dizzy from so

many turns; at moments it seemed to me that I was delirious. During those three hours I broke into perspiration and
dried out three times. Now and then I was pierced to the
heart with the deepest, most venomous pain at the thought
that ten years would go by, and twenty years, and forty
years, and even after forty years I would recall with shud-
dering humiliation these dirtiest, most ludicrous, most terrible minutes of my entire life. No one could possibly
inflict upon himself a more unconscionable, more voluntary humiliation, and I fully realized this, yet I continued to
pace from table to stove and back.

Oh, if you only knew what feelings and ideas I am capable of, how cultivated I am! I thought at moments, mentally addressing the sofa where my enemies sat. But my
enemies behaved as if I were not in the room at all. Once,
only once, they turned to me, and that was when Zverkov
began to speak about Shakespeare, and I burst into derisive
laughter. I snorted so deliberately and viciously that they
stopped their conversation all at once and silently, seriously, without laughing, watched me for a minute or two,
as I paced along the wall from table to stove, *paying them
no attention*. But nothing came of it. They did not address
me, and abandoned me again two minutes later. The clock
struck eleven.

"Gentlemen," cried Zverkov, rising from the sofa.
"Now we shall all go *there*."

"Of course, of course!" they echoed.

I turned sharply toward Zverkov. I was so exhausted, so
broken, that I was ready to cut my throat, anything, only to
put an end to it! I was shaking with fever; my hair, which
had been soaked with perspiration, clung to my temples
and forehead.

"Zverkov! I beg your forgiveness!" I said harshly and
decisively. "Yours too, Ferfichkin. And everyone's,
everyone's—I insulted you all!"

"A-ah! A duel's no joke!" Ferfichkin hissed venomously.

His words slashed painfully across my heart.

"No, it isn't the duel I am afraid of, Ferfichkin! I am ready to fight you tomorrow, after we're reconciled. Indeed, I insist on it, and you cannot refuse. I want to prove to you that I am not afraid of a duel. You will fire first, and I shall fire into the air."

"Playing games with himself," said Simonov.

"He's simply off his head!" responded Trudolyubov.

"Let us pass, will you, get out of the way! . . . Well, what do you want?" Zverkov replied contemptuously. They were all red-faced; their eyes glittered; they had drunk a good deal.

"I ask for your friendship, Zverkov, I insulted you, but . . ."

"Insulted? You! In-sulted me! I'll have you know, dear sir, that you can never under any circumstances *insult me!*"

"That's enough from you, get out of the way!" Trudolyubov said with finality. "Let's go."

"Olympia is mine, gentlemen, that's agreed!" cried Zverkov.

"Agreed! We won't dispute it!" they answered, laughing.

I stood there, spat upon, demolished. The company was noisily piling out of the room. Trudolyubov struck up some silly song. Simonov stayed behind for a fraction of a second to tip the waiters. I suddenly approached him.

"Simonov! Let me have six rubles!" I asked with desperate determination.

He stared at me with extreme astonishment, his eyes dull. He was also drunk.

"You aren't coming *there* with us?"

"Yes, I am!"

"I have no money!" he said curtly and went toward the door with a contemptuous smile.

I seized him by his overcoat. It was a nightmare.

"Simonov! I saw that you have money, why do you refuse me? Am I a scoundrel? Beware of refusing me: if only you knew, if only you knew why I ask for it! Everything depends on it, my whole future, all my plans...."

Simonov took out the money and all but threw it at me.

"Take it, if you are so shameless!" he said mercilessly and hurried to catch up with the others.

I remained alone for a moment. Disorder, remnants of food, a broken wineglass on the floor, spilled wine, cigarette butts, drunken delirium in my head, tormenting misery in my heart, and, finally, the waiter who had seen and heard everything and now stared into my eyes with curiosity.

"I must go *there!*" I exclaimed. "Either they will all fall down on their knees and plead for my friendship, embracing my legs, or ... or I will slap Zverkov!"

V

"SO HERE it is, here it is at last, the confrontation with reality," I muttered, running headlong down the stairs. "No, this is no longer a vision of the Pope leaving Rome and departing for Brazil; it isn't the ball on Lake Como!"

You're a scoundrel, flashed through my mind, if you laugh at it now.

"What if I am!" I cried, answering myself. "Everything's lost now, anyway!"

They were nowhere to be seen. But it didn't matter: I knew where they had gone.

At the entrance stood a solitary night coachman, wrapped in a coarse peasant coat, all of him powdered over with the still falling wet and seemingly warm snow. The air was close and steamy. The little shaggy piebald nag was also powdered with snow, and coughing. I remember this very clearly. I rushed toward the rough-hewn sled; but just as I was raising my foot to get in, the memory of how Simonov had given me the six rubles hit me with full force, and I collapsed into the sled like a heavy sack.

"Oh, no! There is a lot that must be done to make up for it all!" I cried. "But I will make up for it or else die on the spot this very night. Go, driver!"

We started. My head was in a whirl:

They will not beg for my friendship on their knees. That's a mirage, a cheap mirage, disgusting, romantic—a fantasy, no different from the ball on Lake Como. And therefore I must slap Zverkov. It is my duty to slap him. And so, resolved. I'm flying there to slap him.

"Hurry, driver!"

The coachman tugged at the reins.

I'll slap him the moment I come in. Should I say a few words first, as an introduction? No! I shall simply come in and slap him. They will all be sitting in the drawing room, and he'll be on the sofa with Olympia. Damned Olympia! She once laughed at my face and refused me. I'll drag her by the hair and twist Zverkov's ears. No, better take him by one ear and lead him by the ear around the room. They may all fall upon me and hit me and throw me out. In fact, they're sure to. Let them! Still, I will have slapped him first. The initiative will be mine; and according to the code of honor, that is the main thing. He'll be branded with shame, and no amount of blows can wash away a slap, nothing but a duel. He'll have to fight. Very well, let them beat me up. Let them, they know nothing of nobility! Trudolyubov will hit hardest—he's so strong. Ferfichkin will sneak up from the side; he'll clutch me by the hair, I'm sure he will. But let them, let them! I am ready. Their sheeps' brains will be forced, at last, to realize the tragic element in it all! When they drag me to the door, I'll shout to them that they're not worth my little finger.

"Hurry, driver, hurry!" I shouted to the coachman so savagely that it made him start and crack his whip.

We'll duel at dawn, that's decided. I'm through with my post at the department. Yesterday Ferfichkin said "*le*partment" instead of "department." But where can I get the revolvers? Nonsense! I'll take an advance on my salary and buy them. And what about the powder and bullets? That's the second's task. But how will I manage it all before dawn? And where will I find a second? I have no acquaintances.... "Nonsense!" I cried, whipping myself up still more. Nonsense! I can ask the first man I meet in the street, and he will have to be my second, just as he would have to save a drowning person from the water. I must assume the possibility of the most eccentric eventualities. Why, even if I should ask the director himself tomorrow to be my second, he'd have to accept out of a sense of chivalry, and keep it confidential, too! Anton Antonych...

The fact is that at those very moments I was more clearly and vividly aware of the revolting absurdity of my imaginings and the entire reverse side of the medal than anyone else in the world could have been. And yet...

"Hurry, driver, hurry, you rascal, hurry!"

"Ah, sir!" said the son of the land.

I felt a sudden chill.

Wouldn't it be better...wouldn't it be better...to go straight home? Oh, God! Why, why did I invite myself to that dinner yesterday! But no, it is impossible! And the three-hour walk from table to stove? No, it's they, they, and no one else who must repay me for that walk! They must wipe out that disgrace!

"Get on, driver!"

And what if they take me to the police? They won't dare. They'll be afraid of a scandal. And what if Zverkov refuses to duel with me out of contempt? He's almost certain to. But then I'll prove to them.... I'll rush down to the stage post when he's leaving tomorrow, I'll grab him by the leg, I'll pull off his coat as he climbs into the coach. I'll sink my teeth into his hands, I'll bite him. "Look, every-body, what a desperate man can be driven to!" Let him hit me on the head, with all the rest of them attacking from behind. I'll shout to everybody: "Look at this pup who's going off to charm Circassian maidens with my spittle on his face!"

Naturally, after that everything will be finished! The department will vanish from the face of the earth. I'll be seized, I'll be tried, I'll be kicked out of my job and sent to prison, to Siberia, to exile. No matter! Fifteen years later, when they release me from jail, I'll drag myself after him in rags, a pauper. I'll seek him out in some provincial town. He'll be happily married. He'll have a grown-up daughter.... I'll say: "Look, beast, look at my sunken cheeks and my tatters! I've lost everything—my career, my happiness, art, science, a *beloved woman,* and all because of you. Here are the revolvers. I have come to discharge my revolver, and...forgive you." Then I will fire into the air, and no one will ever hear of me again....

I even broke into tears, though all the while I knew with perfect clarity that this was all from Silvio and from Lermontov's *Masquerade*[22] And I suddenly felt dreadfully ashamed, so ashamed that I halted the sled, climbed out, and stepped into the deep snow in the middle of the street. The coachman looked at me with astonishment and sighed.

What was I to do? I could neither go there—the affair was too absurd; nor could I leave the matter as it was, because then it would be..."Lord! How can I ignore it! After such insults! No!" I cried, throwing myself again into the sled. "It's predetermined, it is fate! Go on, faster, faster!"

In my impatience I punched the driver on the neck with my fist.

"What's the matter with you? What are you hitting me for?" the wretched little peasant cried, but nevertheless he whipped his nag until she began to kick at him with her hind legs.

The wet snow fell in large flakes. I unbuttoned my coat, ignoring it. I forgot everything else, for I had decided irrevocably on the slap, and felt with horror that *now it was bound to happen,* right away, at once, and *nothing in the world* could stop it. The lonely street lamps flickered gloomily in the snowy murk like torches at a funeral. Snow got into my coat, under my jacket, under my tie, and melted there. I did not cover myself; no matter, everything was already lost anyway! At last we drove up. I jumped out, almost beside myself, ran up the steps, and began to hammer on the door with my fists and feet. My legs suddenly grew weak, especially in the knees. Someone opened quickly, as if they had known I would arrive. (Indeed, Simonov had told them that someone else might come, for this was a place where visits had to be announced in advance and where precautions generally had to be taken. It was one of those "fashionable shops" of the time, which have long since been eradicated by the police. During the day it was in fact a shop; and in the evening those with proper recommendations were able to visit the establishment.) I walked rapidly through the dark shop into the familiar parlor, illuminated by a single candle. I stopped in bewilderment: no one was there.

"But where are they?" I asked someone.

Naturally, they had already gone their separate ways....

Before me stood a person with a stupid smile, the proprietress herself, who knew me slightly. A moment later the door opened and another person came in.

Paying no attention to anything, I paced the room and, I believe, talked to myself. I was like a man saved from death, and felt it joyously with my whole being. For I would have slapped him, I surely, surely would have slapped him! But now they were not here and...everything vanished, everything was different!...I looked around me. I still could not grasp it. Mechanically I glanced at the girl who had just entered: a fresh, young, rather pale face with straight dark eyebrows and grave, as though slightly astonished, eyes. I liked her immediately; I would have hated her if she had smiled. I looked at her more attentively and almost with an effort; my mind had not yet cleared. There was something simple and kind in that face, but oddly serious. I am certain that all of this was to her disadvantage there, and none of those fools had taken notice of her. But then, she could not be called a beauty, although she was tall, strong, and well built. She was dressed very simply. Something nasty stirred within me; I approached her directly....

By chance, I caught sight of my face in a mirror. My overwrought face seemed to me extraordinarily repulsive: pale, furious, mean, with disheveled hair. It doesn't matter, I'm glad, I thought. Yes, precisely, I am glad that I will seem repulsive to her; it pleases me....

VI

SOMEWHERE BEHIND a partition a clock wheezed as if someone were pressing on it hard, throttling it. After an unnaturally prolonged wheezing, there followed a thin, nasty, and unexpectedly hurried chime—as if someone had suddenly leaped forward. It struck two. I awakened, although I had not been asleep, but lay there in a semiconscious state.

The room, narrow, cramped, and low-ceilinged, dominated by an enormous wardrobe and littered with cartons, rags, and all sorts of shabby clothing, was almost entirely dark. The candle end on the table across the room was guttering, flaring up faintly from time to time. A few moments, and there would be total darkness.

It did not take me long to return to consciousness. Everything came back to my mind at once, without any effort, as though it had just been waiting to pounce upon me once again. And even as I dozed, there had still remained a constant spot somewhere in my memory that refused to be forgotten and around which my vague dreams circled heavily. But strangely, all that had happened to me that day seemed now, on awakening, to belong to a distant, distant past, as if I had long, long ago left all of it behind.

My mind was in a daze. Something seemed to float over me, brushing against me, exciting and troubling me. Anguish and spleen surged up again and again and sought an outlet. Suddenly I saw beside me two open eyes, examining me with steady curiosity. Their gaze was coldly indifferent, sullen, a total stranger's; it oppressed me.

A gloomy thought came to my mind and ran through my whole body with the peculiarly odious sensation one gets on entering a damp and moldy underground cellar. It seemed somehow unnatural that those eyes had only now taken to studying me. I also recalled that in the course of two hours I had not said a single word to this being, and had not deemed it necessary; in fact, I had even enjoyed this. But now, all at once, I realized with utmost clarity the whole absurdity, as loathsome as a spider, of fornication, which rudely and shamelessly, without love, begins directly with that which consummates true love. We looked at one another like that for a long time, but she did not lower her eyes before mine, and their expression never changed, which in the end gave me an eerie feeling.

"What is your name?" I asked curtly, to put a quick end to the staring.

"Liza," she replied, almost in a whisper, but somehow altogether ungraciously, and looked away.

I was silent a while.

"What weather we have today ... snow ... vile!" I said, almost to myself, miserably, putting my hand under my head and looking at the ceiling.

She did not answer. The whole business was sickening.

"Are you a native here?" I asked a minute later, almost angrily, turning my head slightly toward her.

"No."

"Where from?"

"Riga," she answered reluctantly.

"German?"

"Russian."

"Have you been here long?"

"Where?"

"In this house."

"Two weeks." She spoke more and more curtly. The candle went out altogether and I could no longer distinguish her face.

"Have you a mother and father?"

"Yes ... no ... I have."

"Where are they?"

"Back there ... in Riga."

"Who are they?"

"Oh, just ..."

"Just what? What are they?"

"Townsfolk."

"You've always lived with them?"

"Yes."

"How old are you?"

"Twenty."

"Why did you leave them?"

"Just so. ..."

This "just so" meant "leave me alone, stop bothering." We fell silent.

God knows why I did not leave. I felt increasingly depressed and wretched. The events of that whole day began to flow in confusion through my mind, independent of my will. I suddenly recalled a scene I had witnessed in the street that morning as I had hurried anxiously to work.

"Some men were carrying out a coffin today and almost dropped it." I suddenly spoke aloud, almost accidentally, without intending to start a conversation.

"A coffin?"

"Yes, on Sennaya Street; they were bringing it out of a cellar."

"A cellar?"

"Not a cellar, but a basement floor . . . oh, you know . . . downstairs . . . out of a brothel. . . . Such filth all around . . . peelings, garbage . . . stench . . . it was disgusting."

Silence.

"Nasty day for a funeral!" I started again, just to break the silence.

"Why nasty?"

"Snow, slush. . . ." I yawned.

"What's the difference," she said suddenly after a pause.

"No, it's vile. . . ." (I yawned again.) "The gravediggers must have been cursing, getting wet in the snow. And there was probably water in the grave."

"Water in the grave? Why?" she asked with an odd curiosity, but speaking still more harshly and curtly than before. Something suddenly began to goad me on.

"Naturally, there was water in the pit, at least six inches. You cannot ever dig a dry grave in the Volkovo cemetery."

"Why?"

"What do you mean why? The place is swampy. All bog. They bury them right in the water. I've seen it myself . . . many times. . . ."

(I had never seen it and had really never been in Volkovo. I'd merely heard about it.)

"Does it really make no difference to you if you die?"

"Why should I die?" she answered, as if defending herself.

"Well, someday you will, and you'll die just like that other one. She was also.... She died of consumption."

"A whore would have died in a hospital...." (She knows all about it already, I thought. And she said "whore," not "woman.")

"She owed money to the madam," I said, spurred on more and more by the argument. "And she worked for her almost to the very end, although she had consumption. The cabmen around there were talking to the soldiers, telling them about it. Her old acquaintances, most likely. They laughed. They even talked of having a drink in her memory at the tavern." (I invented much of this too.)

Silence. Deep silence. She did not even stir.

"You think it's better, then, to die at the hospital?"

"What difference does it make?... And why should I die, anyway," she added irritably.

"If not now, then later."

"Well, then, so it will be later...."

"Sure, you can say that now! You're young, good-looking, fresh—and so you're valued accordingly. But a year of this life, and you won't be the same, you'll wither."

"A year?"

"In any case, after a year your price will drop," I went on, gloating maliciously. "And you will go from here to another house, a bit cheaper. And in another year there will be a third one, still lower down. In seven years or so you'll come down to a basement on Sennaya. And that won't be the worst of it. The real trouble will come if you get sick besides, say a weakness in the chest... or a cold, or something. In this kind of life an illness is no joke. It takes hold of you and you can't get rid of it. And so you'll die."

"Well, then, I'll die," she snapped back altogether angrily, with a quick movement.

"It's a pity, though."

"A pity for whom?"

"A pity to lose life."

Silence.

"Were you engaged to someone? Eh?"

"What's that to you?"

"Oh, I'm not questioning you. It's nothing to me. What are you sore about? Of course, you may have had your troubles. What's it to me? Just the same, I'm sorry."

"For whom?"

"For you."

"No need to..." she whispered barely audibly and stirred again.

This provoked me at once. What! I'd been so gentle with her, and she....

"What do you think, now? You're on the right path, eh?"

"I don't think anything."

"That's the whole trouble, that you don't think. Wake up while there's still time. And there is time. You're still young and pretty. You could fall in love, get married, be happy...."

"Not everybody who's married is happy," she rapped out harshly, as before.

"Not everybody, of course. Yet it's much better than here. Incomparably better. And if there's love, you can do without happiness too. Even with sorrow, life is sweet; it's good to be alive, no matter how. And what do you have here, but... stench. Phew!"

I turned to her with loathing. I was no longer reasoning coldly. I had begun to feel what I was saying and spoke vehemently. I was already longing to express the *cherished little ideas* I had nurtured in my corner. Something was suddenly fired in me, a kind of purpose "appeared" before me.

"Never mind that I am here, I'm no example to you. I may be even worse than you. And incidentally, I was drunk when I came," I nevertheless hastened to justify myself. "Besides, a man is no example for a woman. It's quite another matter. I may be fouling and besmirching myself, but I am nobody's slave. I'm here one minute, and gone the next. I shake it off, and I'm a different man. But you? You are a slave from the very first. Yes, a slave! You've given up everything, your whole freedom. And later you may want to break these chains, but no: they'll bind you ever faster. That's the kind of an accursed chain it is. I know it. I will not speak of other things, you may not even understand them, but tell me: aren't you already in debt to your madam? There, you see!" I added, although she did not answer but listened to me silently, with her whole being. "There's your chain! You'll never buy your way out. They'll make sure of that. It's like selling your soul to the devil. . . .

"Besides, I . . . for all you know, perhaps I'm just as miserable as you, and also throw myself into this filth deliberately, out of misery. After all, others drink to drown their sorrow; and I come here. . . . Now tell me, what's good about this place? Take you and me. We were . . . together . . . just before, and didn't say a word to one another all the time. And it was only afterwards that you began to look at me—like a wild thing; and I did the same. Is that how people love? Is that how a human being should come together with another? It's disgusting, that's all it is!"

"Yes!" she agreed, sharply and hastily. I was, in fact, surprised by the hastiness of this *yes*. So the same idea must have passed through her mind when she was scrutinizing me before? So she was already capable of some thought? . . . The devil take it, I thought to myself, almost rubbing my hands, that's interesting—a kind of *kinship*. Surely, I couldn't fail to get the best of such a young soul! . . .

What excited me most was the sport of it.

She turned her head closer to mine and in the darkness it seemed to me that she propped herself up on her arm.

Perhaps she was examining me again. I was sorry I could not see her eyes. I heard her deep breathing.

"Why did you come here?" I began, with a certain sense of power now.

"Oh, just so . . ."

"But think how good it would be to be living in your father's house! Warm and free; your own nest."

"And what if it was worse than that?"

I must find the right tone, I thought; sentiment, it seems, won't work here.

But this merely flashed through my mind. I swear, she really interested me. Besides, I was somehow affected and in the right mood. After all, bluff and real emotion exist so easily side by side.

"Who can tell!" I hastened to reply. "All sorts of things happen. But I'm sure somebody has hurt you, and they're more guilty before you than you are before *them*. I don't know anything about your past, but a girl like you wouldn't come here of her own free will. . . ."

"What kind of a girl am I?" she whispered just audibly. But I heard.

The devil take it, I thought, I'm flattering her. That's vile. But maybe it's good. . . . She was silent.

"You see, Liza—I'll talk about myself! If I had had a family as a child, I'd be a different man. I think about it often. After all, no matter how bad things are in a family, you're still with your mother and father, not enemies, not strangers. They'll show you some affection at least once a year. At least you know it's your own home. I've grown up without any family; that must be why I've turned out like this . . . without feelings."

I waited again.

I guess she doesn't understand, I thought. It's funny, too: all that moralizing.

"If I were a father and had a daughter, I think I'd love her more than any sons, really," I began from round about, as if talking of someone else, to distract her. I confess, I blushed.

"Why so?" she asked.

So she was listening!

"Well, I don't know, Liza. You see, I knew a certain father who was a hard, stern man. But when it came to his daughter, he kneeled for hours before her, kissing her hands and feet, he couldn't admire her enough. She'd be dancing at a party, and he would stand for five hours on the same spot, never taking his eyes off her. He was crazy about her. I can understand that. She'd be tired at night and go to sleep, and he would wake up and go over to kiss her as she slept and make the sign of the cross over her. He went about in the shabbiest coat himself, he was a miser with everybody else, but for her he'd spend his last kopek; he kept buying her rich presents and knew no greater joy than when she liked his present. A father always loves his daughters more than a mother. Some girls have a jolly life at home! And I, I think I'd never let my daugher marry."

"How's that?" she asked, with a faint smile.

"I'd be jealous, I swear I'd be. How could I let her kiss somebody else? Or love a stranger more than her own father? It hurts even to think of it. Naturally, it's all nonsense; naturally, everybody must come to his senses in the end. But I think I would make myself sick with worrying before I'd let her go: I'd find something wrong with every suitor. And still, I'd end up by letting her marry the man she loved. Because to a father the man his daughter loves will always seem the worst of all. That's how it is. It makes for a lot of trouble in many families."

"Some are glad to sell their daughter rather than let her marry honorably," she said suddenly.

Ah! So that was it!

"That, Liza, happens in those accursed families where there is neither God nor love," I seized upon it heatedly. "And where there is no love, there is no reason. True enough, there are such families, but I'm not talking about them. I guess you didn't see much kindness in your family, that's why you speak like that. You must be really unfortunate. Hm.... But all this happens mostly because of poverty."

"And is it any better among the gentry? Honest folk live decently in poverty too."

"Hm ... yes. Perhaps. But there's also this, Liza: people like to count only their troubles, not the good things in their lives. If they looked properly, they'd see that everybody has his share of happiness allotted to him. But imagine a family where everything goes well, with God's blessing; your husband is good and loves and cherishes you, won't take a step away from you! How good life is in such a family! Even, sometimes, with troubles and with sorrow, but good all the same. Besides, who has no troubles? Perhaps you will get married and *find out for yourself*. But think, let's say, of the early years of marriage to a man you love: the happiness, the happiness of it sometimes! Why, you see it all around. In the beginning even quarrels with the husband end well. Some women, the more they're in love, the more quarrels they'll pick with their husbands. Really, I knew a woman like that. 'I love you so much,' she'd say, 'it's out of love that I torment you, so you'll feel it.' Do you know that it is possible to torment another out of love? It's mostly women that do it, thinking to themselves, 'I'll make it up to him afterwards with all my love, with the tenderest caresses—it doesn't matter if I make him suffer a bit first.' And everybody admires you in the house, everything is sweet and gay and peaceful and honest....

"Then there are some who are jealous. I knew a woman—if her husband stepped out anywhere, she couldn't bear it, she'd run out on the darkest night and hurry, on the quiet, to see: was he in this house, or that, or with some other woman? That's bad, now. And she knows herself it's bad, her heart sinks, she reproaches herself, but

still she loves him, she does it all out of love. And how
sweet it is to make up after a quarrel, to confess to him, or
to forgive him! And both will feel so light-hearted, so
happy—as though they'd just met anew, just gotten married again, as though their love were just beginning. And
no one, no one must know what goes on between husband
and wife if they love one another. Whatever their quarrel,
they shouldn't call even their own mother to judge between them, or complain about each other. They are their
own judges.

"Love is God's mystery and should be hidden from out-
siders' eyes, whatever happens. This makes it holier, better. The husband and the wife respect each other more, and
a great deal is founded on respect. And if there has been
love, if they were married for love, why should love cease?
Isn't it possible to keep it alive? It is a rare case when it's
impossible. Besides, if the husband happens to be a kind
and honest man, how can love pass? It's true, the feeling of
the early married days will pass, but the love that will
come afterwards will be still better. Man and wife will
grow close in spirit; they'll share in common all their do-
ings, they'll have no secrets from each other. And when
children start coming, the hardest times will seem happy,
so long as there is and courage. Work goes like a song,
and even if you have to deny yourself a piece of bread
once in a while for the children's sake, life's full of joy all
the same. After all, they'll love you for it afterwards; so
that you're really saving for your own future.

"The children start growing up, and you feel that you
are setting an example for them; that even when you die,
they'll carry your thoughts and feelings inside them all
their lives, for you've bequeathed them your image, and
they will grow up in your likeness. So you see, this is a
great duty, and how can the mother and father help but
grow closer? Some people say it is a hardship to have children. But who says so? It's a joy from heaven! Do you love

babies, Liza? I love them terribly. You know—imagine a pink little boy suckling your breast. What husband's heart could turn against his wife, seeing her with his child? The baby, rosy, plump, spreads out his arms and legs, luxuriating in your warmth; his little hands and feet are firm like ripe apples, the nails clean and tiny, so tiny they are comical to see, and the eyes look at you as though he already understands everything. And when he suckles, he tugs at your breast with his little hand, playing. His father will come over, and the baby will turn from the breast, bend backward, look at him and laugh—as if it were God knows how funny—then start suckling again. Or else, when the teeth begin to come, he'll take a nip at his mother's breast and look at her out of the corner of his eye: 'See, I bit you!' Isn't this the greatest happiness in the world when the three of them, the husband, wife, and child are together? For such moments, a lot can be forgiven. No, Liza, I suppose one has to learn how to live himself before accusing others!"

That's how I'll get to you, I thought, with just such pictures, although, I swear, I spoke with feeling. And suddenly I blushed. What if she bursts out laughing? Where will I hide then? The idea enraged me. Toward the end of my oration I was really carried away, and now my vanity suffered. The silence lasted. I was on the point of jostling her.

"You somehow..." she began suddenly and broke off.

But I already understood it all: something else was trembling in her voice now, not sharp, not rude and unyielding as before, but something soft and shy, so shy that I was overcome with shame, with guilt before her.

"What?" I asked with tender curiosity.

"Well, you..."

"What?"

"You somehow... it's like out of a book," she said, and something mocking seemed again to come into her voice.

Her remark stung me to the quick. It wasn't what I had expected.

I did not understand that she was deliberately hiding behind a mask of mockery, that this is usually the last subterfuge of people who are shy and chaste of heart in the face of rude, importunate attempts to probe their soul, and who refuse to yield to the very end out of pride and fear of showing their true feelings. I should have guessed it from the very timidity with which she tried, repeatedly, to utter her mocking words, until she finally ventured to speak them. But I did not guess, and a vindictive anger flared up in me.

Just wait now, I thought.

VII

OH, REALLY, Liza, what have books to do with it, when I myself find it loathsome, just seeing it from outside? And not from outside only. All these feelings have now awakened in my heart. . . . Can it be possible, can it be possible that you don't find it loathsome here yourself? No, evidently habit means a lot. The devil knows what habit can do to a person. But can you seriously think that you will never grow old, that you'll always be pretty, that they'll keep you here forever? Not to speak of the vileness here. . . . And yet, let me tell you something about it, about your present way of life: you may be young and good-looking and sweet, with a soul, with feelings, but do you know that when I woke just now, it immediately made me sick to be here with you! A man can come here only when he's drunk. But if you were elsewhere, living like all decent people, I'd probably not only run after you, I'd fall in love with you; not only a word, a glance from you would make me happy; I would be waiting for you at the gates, I'd kneel before you; I'd think of you as my betrothed, and would feel honored, too. I wouldn't dare to have a single unclean thought about you.

"And here—don't I know that I just have to whistle, and, whether you want to or not, you must come with me, and it isn't I who do your will, but you who do mine. The lowliest peasant will hire himself out as a laborer, yet he will not allow himself to be enslaved completely; besides, he knows it's only for a time. And where is the end of your servitude? Just think about it: what are you giving up here? What are you putting into bondage? You're putting your soul into bondage together with your body—your soul, which isn't yours to dispose of! You're giving up your love, to be trampled by every drunk! Love! Why, that's everything, it is a precious jewel, a girl's treasure, that's what love is! To earn that love a man may be ready to offer up his soul, to face death itself. And what's the price of your love now? You're bought, the whole of you, and why should anybody seek your love when he can get everything without it?

"There is no insult to a girl worse than that, do you understand? I've heard it said that they indulge you, stupid girls, they allow you to have lovers here. But that's just fooling, just a sham, a mockery, and you are taken in by it. Does he really have any feelings for you, that lover of yours? I don't believe it. How can he love you when he knows you may be called away from him at any moment. He's a swine, after all that! Does he have the least bit of respect for you? What do you have in common with him? He laughs at you and robs you in addition—that's all his love means! And you're lucky if he doesn't beat you. But perhaps he does. Just ask your lover, if you have one: would he marry you? Why, he'll laugh in your face, if he doesn't spit at you or beat you up—and, for all you know, he may not be worth a broken kopek himself. And what, come to think of it, have you ruined your whole life for? For the coffee they give you here, and the plentiful food? But what is it they're feeding you for? Another woman, an honest one, would choke on the first bite, because she'd know what she was getting it for. You owe money here; well, you'll be in debt to them until the very end, until the guests start rejecting you. And that will happen soon enough, don't count on your youth. Here everything flies posthaste. They'll throw you out. And not simply throw you out, but start picking on you long before; they will reproach you, scold you—as though it wasn't for your madam that you'd given up your health and youth and soul, and gotten nothing in return; as though you'd eaten her out of house and home, as though you'd beggared her and robbed her.

"And don't expect anyone to take your side: the other girls will also turn against you, to get into the madam's good graces, because everybody here's in bondage, they've lost all conscience and compassion long ago. They've fallen to the lowest depths, and nothing on earth is filthier, meaner, more insulting than such abuse. And you'll lose everything in this place, everything you have—your health, your youth, your beauty, and your hopes. At twenty-two you will look thirty-five, and you'll be lucky if you aren't sick, pray to God for that.

"I'll bet you're thinking now that you have it easy—no work, all play! Why, there is no harder work than this in the whole world, and never has been. I would expect you'd cry your very heart out. And when they kick you out of here, you will not dare to say a word; you'll go as though you were the guilty one. You'll go to another place, then a third, then sink still lower, and end up on Sennaya. And there they will start beating you, just so, in passing; that's their kind of pleasantry. There the visitors don't know how to show any kindness without first beating you up. You don't believe it's so disgusting there? Go, take a look sometime, perhaps you'll see it with your own eyes. I saw a woman there one New Year's Day, outside a door. She had been pushed out as a joke by her own kind, to freeze a bit, because she cried too much. And then they locked her out. At nine in the morning she was already dead drunk, disheveled, half-naked, beaten black and blue. Face white with powder, with dark bruises around her eyes, blood running from her nose and teeth: some coachman had just fixed her up.

"She sat on the stone stairs, with some kind of salted fish in her hands. She bawled and wailed about her bitter lot and kept banging the fish on the stairs. Cabbies and drunken soldiers gathered around the steps and teased her. You don't believe you'll be like that yourself? I wouldn't believe it either; but who knows, perhaps ten years, eight years ago that woman with the fish had come here from somewhere, fresh as a cherub, innocent, pure, knowing no evil, blushing at every word. Perhaps she was like you, proud, easily offended, unlike any of the others, looking like a princess and sure what happiness awaited the man who'd fall in love with her and whom she'd love. And you see what it all came to! And what if, at the very moment when she was banging the fish on the dirty stairs, drunk and disheveled, what if she suddenly remembered the old, innocent years in her father's house, when she was still a schoolgirl and the neighbor's son would wait for her in the street and vow that he would love her all his life, that he would share his destiny with her, and they would promise to love each other forever and marry when they both grew up!

"No, Liza, you'll be lucky if you die quickly of consumption somewhere in a basement hole like the one I saw this morning. You say, a hospital? Good if they take you there, but what if the madam still needs you? Consumption isn't like a fever. Those who have it keep hoping to the last and saying they're well. Just reassuring themselves. And what's it to the madam, she only gains by it. Don't worry, it's true; you've sold your soul and you owe money, and so you wouldn't dare to make a sound. And when you're dying, everybody will abandon you—because there's nothing more to be gained from you. What's more, they'll scold you for taking up space for nothing, for not dying quickly enough. You'll beg for a drink of water, and nobody will bring it, and when they do, it will be with a curse: 'When will you croak, you scum? Groaning all the time, not letting people sleep, no guest will even look at you.' It's true, I've heard such words myself. They'll stick you, dying, into the foulest corner in the cellar—dark and damp; what will your thoughts be as you're lying there alone?

"And when you die, a stranger will lay you out in a hurry, grumbling impatiently. No loving hand will touch you, no one will bless you or sigh for you. All they'll be thinking of is how to get rid of you as quickly as possible. They'll buy you a cheap coffin and carry you out as they carried out that poor woman today, and then they'll go off to a tavern to have a drink to your memory. In the grave—nothing but slush and mud and wet snow—who'll bother about the likes of you? 'Let 'er down, Vanyukha. Eh, what a life—goes down even here with her legs up. Wouldn't you know! Take in the ropes, you rascal.' 'Good enough as it is.' 'What d'you mean good enough? Look at her, lying on her side. After all, she was human too, wasn't she? Oh, well, it'll do, shovel in the dirt.'

"They wouldn't even trouble to argue over you. They'll cover up the coffin in a hurry with the wet blue clay, and off to the tavern.... And that's the end of your memory on earth. Others have children, fathers, husbands visiting their grave—and you? Not a tear, not a sigh, not a thought, and no one, no one in the whole wide world will ever come to you. Your name will disappear, as though you'd never lived, as though you'd never been born! Nothing but mud and swamp, enough to make you wish to knock at the coffin lid at night, when the dead rise: 'Let me out, good people, let me out into the light to live a little! I've lived without ever seeing any life, my life was nothing but a dirty rag, it was drunk away in a tavern on Sennaya. Let me out, kind people, to have another try at living in the world! ...'"

I was so carried away by all this eloquence that my own throat was ready to contract in a spasm of emotion, when ... suddenly I broke off, startled, raised myself a little, and bending my head fearfully, began to listen with a beating heart. And there was cause enough for dismay.

I had long felt that I'd churned up her soul and was breaking her heart, and the more certain I was of it, the stronger my desire to attain my purpose as quickly and forcefully as possible. It was the game, the game that excited me; however, not the game alone ...

I knew that I was speaking stiffly, artificially, even bookishly; indeed, I was incapable of speaking otherwise than "like out of a book." But this did not trouble me, for I knew, I sensed, that I'd be understood and that this very bookishness would, perhaps, even help in my effort. But now, having achieved my effect, I was suddenly unnerved. No, never, never before had I been witness to such despair! She lay prone, her face pressed hard into the pillow, which she clutched with both arms. Her breast was torn with suppressed sobs. Her whole young body shuddered as in convulsions. The sobs pent up within her were stifling her, tearing her apart, and suddenly breaking out in cries and moans. At those moments she pressed herself still harder into the pillow: she did not want anyone in the house, not a single living soul, to learn about her torment and tears. She bit the pillow, she bit her hand until it bled (I saw it afterwards), or else, thrusting her fingers into her tangled hair, she would go rigid with effort, holding her breath and clenching her teeth. I began to say something to her, I begged her to calm down, but suddenly I felt I didn't dare.

And in an odd chill, almost in panic, I groped for my things, hurriedly preparing to leave. It was dark: no matter how I tried, I could not finish dressing quickly enough. Suddenly my hand found a box of matches and a candlestick with a whole, still unused candle. The moment the room was lit, Liza sprang up, sat up in bed, and looked at me almost senselessly, with an oddly twisted face and a half-demented smile. I sat down near her and took her hands; she came to herself and made a quick movement toward me, wanting to embrace me, but she did not dare, and quietly bowed her head before me.

"Liza, my friend, I shouldn't have ... forgive me," I began, but she pressed my hands with her fingers so hard that I realized I was saying the wrong thing and fell silent.

"Here is my address, Liza, come to me."

"I'll come ..." she whispered with determination, still without raising her head.

"And now I'll go, goodbye ... until we meet again."

I rose, and she did too. Then, suddenly blushing all over, she started, snatched up a shawl from the chair and threw it over her shoulders, wrapping herself to her very chin. After that she smiled again with that peculiar, pained smile, blushed, and looked up at me with a strange expression. It distressed me; I was in a hurry to leave, to get away.

"Wait," she said suddenly, already in the hallway, at the door, stopping me with her hand on my coat. She quickly put down the candle and hastened off; she had evidently remembered something or wanted to bring something to show me. As she ran, she flushed, her eyes shone, a smile came to her lips. What did it mean? I couldn't help but wait. She returned in a moment, with a glance that seemed to beg forgiveness for something. Altogether, it was no longer the same face, not the same look as before—sullen, distrustful and obstinate. Her glance was now appealing, soft, and at the same time trusting, tender, and timid. Children look like that at people they love very much and

are asking for something. Her eyes were a light hazel—
beautiful eyes, alive, capable of expressing both love and
sullen hatred.

Without explaining anything—as though I were some
higher being who was bound to know everything without
explanations—she held out to me a slip of paper. Her
whole face glowed at that moment with an utterly naive,
almost childlike triumph. I unfolded the paper. It was a letter to her from some medical student or other—a very
high-flown and flowery, but extremely respectful declara-
tion of love. I don't recall the expressions now, but I remember very well that through the grandiloquence you
sensed genuine emotion, which can never be feigned.
When I finished reading, I met her excited, questioning,
and childishly impatient glance. Her eyes were fixed on
my face and she waited eagerly to hear what I would say.
In a few words, hurriedly, but somehow joyously and as if
proud of it, she explained that she had been at a party
somewhere, in a private home, the home of certain "very,
very good people, *family people,* where *they knew nothing
at all as yet,* nothing at all," because, in fact, she was still
new in this place, and only . . . but she had not yet decided
to remain, and would definitely leave, as soon as she repaid
her debt. . . . Well, and there was this student there, he
danced and talked with her all evening, and it turned out
that he had known her in Riga, he knew her when they
were still children; they played together, but that was very
long ago. And he knew her parents too, but he knew nothing, nothing at all about *this,* and didn't suspect anything!
And on the day after the party (three days ago) he sent her
this letter, through a girl friend with whom she had gone
there . . . and . . . well, that was all.

She lowered her sparkling eyes with a kind of shyness
when she had finished her story.

Poor thing, she kept that student's letter as a precious
jewel, and she ran to show me this one precious possession,

not wanting me to leave without learning that she too was loved honestly and sincerely, that she too was treated with respect. Most probably this letter was fated to remain in her box without consequences. But all the same, I am certain that she would cherish it throughout her life as a treasure, as her pride and justification. And now, at such a moment, she herself recalled that letter and brought it to me, to boast naively, to restore herself in my eyes, so that I too would see it, and express my appreciation. I said nothing, pressed her hand, and left. I was too anxious to get away.... I walked all the way home, although the wet snow was still tumbling down in huge flakes. I was exhausted, crushed, bewildered. But the truth was already beginning to glimmer through the bewilderment. The ugly truth!

VIII

IT WAS some time, however, before I consented to face this truth. Awakening in the morning after several hours of deep, leaden sleep and instantly recalling all of the previous day, I was, in fact, amazed at my *sentimentality* with Liza, at all those "horrors and pities" of last night. "An attack of old woman's nerves, phew!" I decided. "And why the devil did I give her my address? What if she comes? Although, why not, let her come: it doesn't matter...." But, clearly, the chief, the foremost thing now was something else: I had to hurry and at all cost save my reputation in the eyes of Zverkov and Simonov. This was the most important thing. In fact, I soon forgot Liza altogether in the concerns of that morning.

First of all I had to repay last night's debt to Simonov

without delay. I resolved on desperate means—borrowing fifteen rubles from Anton Antonych. As luck would have it, he was in a most excellent mood that morning and immediately let me have it, at the first request. I was so overjoyed that, as I signed the promissory note with a sort of devil-may-care flourish, I told him *very casually* that I'd been "out celebrating with friends the other night at the Hôtel de Paris; seeing off an old comrade—even, you might say, a childhood friend. And, you understand, he is accustomed to a fast life, terribly spoiled—well, naturally, of good family, with a considerable fortune, a brilliant career, witty, charming, carries on with those ladies, you know; we drank 'half a dozen' too much, and..." And wouldn't you know—all of this was spoken lightly, nonchalantly, with the air of a man well-pleased with himself.

When I came home, I immediately wrote a letter to Simonov.

To this day I recall with admiration the truly gentlemanly, good-humored, candid tone of my letter. Smoothly, with dignity, and most important, entirely without superfluous words, I took the blame for everything upon myself. I excused myself, "if I may still attempt any excuses," by saying that, entirely unaccustomed as I was to alcohol, I had become inebriated from the first glass, which I had (supposedly) drunk before their arrival, while waiting for them from five to six at the Hôtel de Paris. I apologized chiefly to Simonov and begged him to transmit my explanations to all the others, and particularly to Zverkov, whom, "I recall as in a dream," I seemed to have insulted. I added that I would have called upon each of them myself, but my head ached and, still worse, I was too embarrassed. I was especially pleased by the "lightness," even carelessness (kept, however, to proper limits) of style which flowed from my pen and, better than any possible arguments, immediately conveyed that I regarded "all that unpleasantness last night" with considerable nonchalance, that I was not at all, not in the slightest crushed, as those gentlemen must have thought, but, on the contrary, regarded everything as it should be regarded by any calmly self-respecting gentleman. "A decent man," as it were, "may slip once in a while."

It even has a kind of aristocratic playfulness, doesn't it? I thought admiringly, as I reread the note. And all because I am an eduated and a cultivated man! Others in my place wouldn't know how to extricate themselves, and I did, and am having fun again, and all because I am "an educated and cultivated man of our time." But come to think of it, perhaps that business yesterday did happen just because of the wine. Hm . . . well, no, not really because of the wine. I never did have anything to drink while waiting for them from five to six. I lied to Simonov. I lied shamelessly. Yet I am not ashamed, even now. . . .

But, anyway, to hell with it! The main thing is that I've disentangled myself.

I enclosed six rubles in the letter, sealed it, and prevailed upon Apollon to take it to Simonov. When he learned that the envelope contained money, he became more respectful and consented to deliver it. In the evening I went out for a stroll. My head still ached and reeled from yesterday's events. As the evening advanced and the dusk gathered, my emotions, and with them my thoughts, kept changing and growing ever more confused. Something would not die down within me, in the depths of my heart and my conscience; it refused to die down and scalded me with anguish. I jostled my way chiefly through the most populous, commercial streets—Meshchanskaya, Sadovaya, along Yusupov Gardens. I was usually particularly fond of strolling down these streets at twilight, just when they became most crowded with all sorts of pedestrians—workers and tradesmen on the way home after a day's toil, with anxious, almost angry faces. I liked precisely this cheap bustle, this blatantly prosaic air. This time, however, all that bustling crowd irritated me still more. I could not get control of myself, could not discover any hint of what was troubling me. Something kept rising and rising within me, endlessly, painfully, and wouldn't settle down. I came home altogether upset, as if some crime were weighing on my heart.

I was continually tormented by the thought that Liza would come. It seemed strange to me that, of all the memories of the preceding day, her memory tormented me with special force, somehow apart from all the rest. I had already managed to forget the rest by evening, I shrugged it off and was still completely pleased with my letter to Simonov. But with regard to Liza I was no longer pleased. As though it were she alone who troubled me. What if she comes? I kept asking myself. Well, what of it, let her come. Hm. It will be rotten, though—if only because she'll see how I live. I posed before her yesterday as such a ... hero ... and now, hm! It's rotten, though, that I've let myself go so badly. The place is so dismal. And I dared to go to dinner yesterday in such clothes! And my oilcloth-covered sofa, with the stuffing coming out of it! And my robe, which doesn't even cover me properly! Tatters... And she will see it all; and she'll see Apollon. That swine will probably insult her. He'll pick on her to humiliate me. And I will, naturally, go into a funk, as usual: I'll simper and fuss before her, and wrap myself in my robe and smile and lie. Ugh, the vileness! But that is not the worst of it! There's something even worse, nastier, lower—yes, lower! I will again put on that unconscionable, lying mask!...

I flared up at this thought: Why unconscionable? What's unconscionable about it? I spoke sincerely last night. I too felt genuine emotion—I remember it. What I sought was precisely to awaken noble emotions in her.... What if she cried a little? It's good, it will produce a beneficent effect....

And yet I could not calm down.

All that evening, even when I had come home, already past nine o'clock, when Liza could no longer be expected, she still haunted me and, what is more, appeared before my mind's eye always in the same position. Of all the moments of the previous night, one stayed with me most vividly—the moment when I lit the match and caught sight of her pale, twisted face, her tormented glance. And that pitiful, unnatural, crooked smile! But I still did not know then that even after fifteen years I would recall Liza precisely with that pathetic, crooked, unnecessary smile on her face at that moment.

On the following day I was again ready to dismiss it all as nonsense, the product of overactive nerves, and above all, an *exaggeration*. I was continually aware of this weakness of mine and sometimes feared it. "I exaggerate everything, that's my trouble," I repeated to myself hourly. And yet, "yet Liza will perhaps come, after all." This was the constant refrain to all my speculations during those days. It worried me so greatly that it drove me to occasional fits of rage. "She'll come! She's sure to come!" I would exclaim, frantically pacing my room. "If not today, then tomorrow, but she is sure to seek me out! The damned romanticism of all these *pure hearts!* The vileness, the stupidity, the narrowness of these 'rotten sentimental souls'! Wouldn't she understand? How could she fail to understand? . . ." But at this point I'd stop in utter confusion.

And how few, how few words were needed, I thought in passing, how little idyllic sentiment (feigned sentiment, at that, bookish and artificial), to turn a whole human soul at once according to my will. Such innocence! Such virgin soil!

At moments I was tempted to go to her myself, "to tell her everything" and persuade her not to come to me. But at this thought such fury would rise up within me that, it seemed to me, I'd crush that "damned Liza" if she were suddenly beside me, I would insult her, spit on her, throw her out, strike her!

Nevertheless, one day went by, another, a third. She did not come, and I began to calm down. I felt especially reassured and emboldened after nine in the evening. Indeed, I'd even take to dreaming, quite pleasantly. For example, I'd see myself saving Liza, precisely through her visits to me and my talks with her. . . . I would develop her mind and educate her. And finally I'd notice that she loved me, loved me passionately. I would pretend I did not see it (I didn't know why I would pretend; simply, I guess, to make it more interesting). At last, embarrassed, beautiful, trembling and sobbing, she would throw herself at my feet, saying that I was her savior and that she loved me more than anything in the world. I would be astonished, but . . . "Liza," I'd say, "do you really imagine that I've never noticed your love? I saw everything, guessed it all, but I dared not make the first step and claim your heart, because I had influenced you and was afraid that you would, out of gratitude, deliberately force yourself to respond to my love, that you would forcibly evoke within yourself an emotion which perhaps did not exist. And this I did not want, for it would be . . . despotic. . . . It would be indelicate (in short, I'd talk myself into some sort of European, George Sandian, incredibly noble refinement . . .'). But now, now—you are mine, you are my creation, you are pure and beautiful, you are my beautiful wife."

> *And enter my home openly and freely—*
> *Full mistress of it all!*[23]

And then we'd start a happy life, we would travel abroad, and so on, and so forth. In a word, I'd go on in this vein until I myself would be nauseated, and would end by sticking my tongue out at my own self.

Anyway, they wouldn't let her out, the "nasty scum"!

I'd think. I don't believe they're allowed to go out much, especially in the evening (for some reason I felt certain that she must come in the evening, and precisely at seven o'clock). However, she said that she had not yet bound herself to them entirely, she has some special privileges. That means—hm! The devil take it, she'll come, she's sure to come!

Luckily I was distracted at the time by Apollon's rude antics. He drove me out of patience altogether! He was the bane of my existence, a punishment inflicted upon me by Providence. We had been squabbling constantly for several years, and I hated him. Lord, how I hated him! I think I've never hated anyone in my entire life as I hated him, especially at certain moments. He was an elderly man, extremely dignified, who engaged in tailoring part of the time. But for some unknown reason he despised me beyond all measure and looked down upon me with intolerable disdain. However, he looked down on everyone. A single glance at that head with its slicked-down flaxen hair, that lock which he brushed up over his forehead and nursed with applications of vegetable oil, that self-righteous mouth, always folded into a pious V—and you felt you were before a creature who had never entertained the slightest doubt about himself. He was pedantic to the highest degree, the worst pedant I have ever met on earth, and with a sense of self-importance that might have been appropriate only perhaps to an Alexander of Macedon. He was enamored of every button on his clothes, every nail on his fingers—yes, enamored, and he looked it! He treated me despotically, spoke to me most sparingly, and whenever he happened to glance at me, he regarded me with a steady, majestically arrogant and invariably mocking look, which often drove me to distraction. He executed his duties with the air of doing me the greatest favor. But then, he did almost nothing for me, and did not even deem himself obliged to do anything. Undoubtedly, he considered me the greatest fool on earth, and if he "kept me on," it was solely because he could get a monthly wage from me. He consented to "do nothing" for me for seven rubles a month. A good many of my sins will surely be forgiven because of him. At times my hatred would reach such a point that his very walk would be enough to throw me into virtual convulsions. But the most repellent thing about him was his lisp. I believe his tongue was rather longer than normal, or something of the sort, for he always lisped and simpered and seemed inordinately proud of it, imagining that this lent him enormous dignity. He spoke in slow, measured tones, with hands folded behind his back and eyes lowered to the ground. He infuriated me especially when he'd begin to read the Psalter in his cubbyhole behind the partition. I fought many battles with him over that reading. But he was terribly fond of reading aloud in the evenings, in a slow, even singsong, as if reading over the dead. Interestingly enough, this was what he ended up with—he now hires out to read the Psalter over the dead, an occupation he combines with the extermination of rats and the manufacture of shoe polish.

In those years, however, I could not bring myself to dismiss him, as though he were a chemical component of my existence. Besides, he himself would never, never under any circumstances have agreed to leave me. As for me, I could not live in a furnished room; my lodgings were my private domain, my shell, the case into which I withdrew from all mankind. Apollon, the devil knows why, seemed to be a part of these lodgings, and for seven long years I was unable to throw him out.

It was unthinkable, for instance, to withhold his wages for even two or three days. He'd start such a business that I wouldn't know where to hide. But at that time I was so embittered with everyone that I decided, heaven knows why or to what purpose, to *punish* Apollon and hold back his wages for two weeks. I had long intended to do this—for about two years, in fact—solely to teach him not to be so supercilious with me, to prove to him that, if I wanted, I could always withhold his wages. I resolved to say nothing to him about it, to be deliberately silent, in order to subdue his pride and force him to be the first to broach the subject. Then I would take the seven rubles from the drawer and show him that I had it, that I had purposely laid it aside, but "did not wish, did not wish, simply did not wish to pay him his wage, did not wish it because I *chose not to,*" because this was "my will as his master," because he was disrespectful, because he was rude; but that if he asked for it with due respect, I might perhaps relent and give it to him; otherwise he'd wait two more weeks, three weeks, a whole month...

But, angry as I was, he was the victor. I broke down before four days were out. He began as he usually did in such cases, for such cases had already occurred before, had been attempted (and, I must note, I knew all this beforehand, I knew his foul tactics by heart). He would start by fixing me with an extremely severe stare that lasted many minutes, especially when he was meeting me or seeing me out of the house. If I held out and pretended not to notice these stares, he would go on to further tortures, still maintaining silence. He would suddenly enter my room for no good reason, moving slowly and smoothly, stop at the door, put one hand behind his back and fix me, as I was reading or pacing the room, with his stare, which this time was not so much severe as utterly derisive. If I asked him what he wanted, he would not answer but go on staring straight at me for several seconds longer; then, compressing his lips in a special way, he would turn slowly, with a meaningful air, and slowly retire to his room. In two hours or so he would suddenly leave his room again and present himself before me. At times, in a rage, I would no longer ask him what he wanted but would sharply and imperiously raise my head and stare back at him. We'd stare at one another in this way for two minutes or so; at last he'd turn with unhurried dignity and retire once again for a couple of hours.

If all of this did not sufficiently edify me and I continued to rebel, he would suddenly begin to sigh as he looked at me—long, deep sighs that seemed to plumb the full depth of my moral degeneration. And, naturally, it would end up in his total triumph: I raved and shouted, but was nevertheless compelled to yield on the point of contention.

But this time, at the very start of the usual maneuver of "stern glances," I immediately flew into a rage. I was already under too much strain, even without him.

"Wait!" I shouted, beside myself, as he slowly and silently turned, one hand behind his back, to withdraw to his room. "Wait! Come back. Come back, I say!" I must have roared so unnaturally that he turned around and began to examine me with some astonishment. Nevertheless, he did not utter a word, and this was what incensed me most of all.

"How dare you enter without asking and stare at me like that? Answer me!"

But after regarding me imperturbably for half a minute, he began to turn again.

"Wait!" I bellowed, rushing up to him. "Don't you move from the spot! There. Now answer me: what did you expect to see here?"

"If there is aught you'd have me do now, my job is to obey," he answered after another pause, simpering in measured tones, raising his eyebrows, and calmly bending his head from one shoulder to the other. And all of this with the most outrageous composure.

"That isn't, that isn't what I'm asking you, you torturer!" I screamed, shaking with rage. "I'll tell you myself, you hangman, what you've come here for. You see I haven't given you your wage, and you're too proud to bow and ask for it. That's why you come here with your stupid stares to punish me, to torture me, and you don't even sus-s-pect, you hangman, how stupid it is, stupid, stupid, stupid!"

He silently began to turn again, but I seized him.

"Listen," I shouted at him. "Here's the money, you see? Here it is!" I took it out of the drawer. "The whole seven rubles, but you will not get it, you will not get it until you come respectfully, to admit your guilt, to beg my pardon. Do you hear!"

"That can never be!" he answered with odd self-assurance.

"It will!" I shouted. "I give you my word of honor, it will!"

"I've nothing to beg your pardon for," he went on, seemingly oblivious of my shouting. " 'Cause it was you who called me 'hangman,' for which I can always lodge a complaint against you at the precinct."

"Go on! Complain!" I roared. "Go now, this very minute, this very second! And all the same you are a hangman! A hangman! A hangman!"

But he merely glanced at me, then turned and, paying no more attention to my calls, sailed off smoothly to his room without a backward look.

If it weren't for Liza, none of this would have happened! I decided to myself. Then, after standing still for a minute, I proceeded with a dignified and solemn air, but also with a slowly and violently beating heart, to his corner behind the screen.

"Apollon," I said quietly and distinctly, but gasping for air. "Go at once, without delay, for the precinct policeman!"

He had meanwhile managed to sit down at his table, put on his glasses, and take up some sewing. But hearing my order, he suddenly snorted with laughter.

"Go at once, this minute! Go, or you can't imagine what will happen!"

"Truly, you're out of your mind," he remarked without even troubling to raise his head, lisping unhurriedly as before, and continuing to thread his needle. "Who's ever seen a man call the authorities against himself? As for scaring me, you're putting yourself out for nothing, 'cause nothing will come of it."

"Go!" I screeched, grabbing his shoulder. Another moment, I felt, and I would strike him.

I did not hear the door from the hallway open quietly and slowly at that moment; someone entered, stopped, and stared at us in perplexity. I glanced up, turned numb with shame, and rushed back to my room. There, clutching my hair with both hands, I leaned my head against the wall and stood motionless in that position.

About two minutes later I heard Apollon's slow footsteps.

"There's a *person* out there, asking for you," he said, looking at me with particular sternness. Then he stepped aside and let in—Liza. He was reluctant to leave and studied us with mocking eyes.

"Get out! Get out!" I commanded him in confusion. At that moment my clock strained, wheezed, and struck seven.

IX

And enter my home openly and freely—
Full mistress of it all!

FROM THE SAME POEM

I STOOD before her, crushed, humiliated, sickeningly ashamed, and, I think, smiling as I struggled desperately to wrap myself in my tattered quilted robe—well, exactly as I had imagined the other day in my fit of depression. Apollon lingered on for two minutes or so and then left, but this did not make things any easier. Worst of all, she also suddenly became embarrassed, more acutely than I ever would have expected. At the sight of me, of course.

"Sit down," I said mechanically and moved up a chair for her by the table, while I sat down on the sofa. She instantly and obediently sat down, gazing at me wide-eyed and evidently expecting something of me. This naive expectation threw me into a rage, but I constrained myself.

She should have tried not to notice anything, as though all was as it should be, but she . . . And I dimly felt that she would pay me dearly *for all this*.

"You've found me in an odd position, Liza," I began, stammering and realizing that this was precisely the wrong way to begin.

"No, no, don't imagine anything!" I cried, seeing her blush suddenly. "I am not ashamed of my poverty. . . . On the contrary, I regard my poverty with pride. I am poor, but honorable. . . . One can be poor but honorable," I muttered. "However . . . Would you like some tea?"

"No . . ." she began.

"Wait!"

I jumped up and hurried off to Apollon. I had to escape somewhere.

"Apollon," I whispered feverishly, hurriedly, throwing him the seven rubles which were still clutched in my fist. "Here are your wages; you see, I'm giving them to you. But in return, you must save me: go to the tavern at once and bring some tea and ten rusks. If you refuse, you'll ruin a man's life! You don't know what kind of woman that is. . . . That's all! You may be imagining something. . . . But you don't know what kind of woman she is! . . ."

Apollon, who had already sat down to his work and had again put on his glasses, first squinted silently at the money without abandoning his needle; then, paying me no attention whatsoever and making no reply, he continued to fuss with the thread, which he was still trying to draw into the needle's eye. I waited for three minutes, standing before him with arms folded à la Napoleon. My temples were wet with perspiration; I was pale, I felt it myself. But thank God, he must have taken pity on me. He finished with his thread, rose deliberately from his seat, slowly pushed away his chair, slowly removed his glasses, slowly counted the money, and finally, asking me over his shoulder whether I wanted a whole portion, he slowly walked out of the room. As I was returning to Liza, the thought occurred to me on the way: wouldn't it be best to run away, just as I was, in my torn robe, no matter where, and let things turn out as they might?

I sat down again. She looked at me anxiously. For several minutes we were silent.

"I'll murder him!" I cried out suddenly, banging my fist on the table so hard that the ink splashed out of the inkwell.

"Ah, what are you saying!" she exclaimed, starting.

"I'll murder him, I'll murder him!" I screeched, hammering on the table, utterly beside myself and at the same time fully realizing how stupid it was to be in such a frenzy.

"You don't know, Liza, what this torturer is doing to me. He is my torturer.... He has gone for some rusks now; he..."

And suddenly I burst into tears. It was a nervous seizure. I was mortified amid the sobs, but could no longer restrain them.

She was frightened. "What is it! What's the matter?" she cried, bustling around me.

"Water, give me some water, over there!" I muttered weakly, totally aware, however, that I could do very well without water and without muttering weakly. But I was *acting,* as it were, to save face, although the fit had been a real one.

She brought me water, looking at me like a lost soul. At that moment Apollon brought in the tea. I suddenly felt that this ordinary and prosaic tea was frightfully inappropriate and trivial after all that had happened, and I blushed. Liza looked at Apollon with something akin to fear. He went out without a glance at us.

"Liza, do you despise me?" I said, looking straight at her, trembling with impatience to learn what she thought.

She was too embarrassed to say anything.

"Drink the tea," I said viciously. I was furious with myself but, naturally, she was the one who would pay. A terrible anger against her surged through my heart; I could have killed her. To avenge myself on her, I swore to myself not to say a single word to her throughout her visit. It's all her fault, I thought.

Our silence lasted about five minutes. The tea stood on the table; we did not touch it. I was so angry that I deliberately refrained from starting first, to make it still more difficult for her; and it was too awkward for her to begin by herself. She glanced at me several times in sad perplexity. I remained obstinately silent. I was, of course, the chief sufferer because I was aware of the revolting meanness of my vicious stupidity, and yet I could not control myself.

"I . . . want to . . . leave that place . . . altogether," she began, in order somehow to break the silence, but poor thing! This was the one subject she should not have broached at that moment, stupid enough as it was, and to a man like me, stupid enough as I was. Yet even my heart was struck with pity for her awkwardness and her unnecessary directness. But something odious immediately suppressed all pity; indeed, it spurred me on still more: let the whole world be damned! Five more minutes went by.

"I am not disturbing you?" She began timidly, just audibly, and made a move to get up.

But at this first glimpse of injured dignity I began to shake with rage, which immediately broke all bounds.

"What did you come here for, will you tell me, please?" I began, gasping for breath and not even considering the logical order of my words. I longed to scream out everything, all at once; I didn't even trouble to think of how to begin.

"Why did you come? Answer me! Answer me!" I cried out, scarcely aware of what I was doing. "I'll tell you, woman, why you came. You came because of my *pathetic* words to you that time. So you got sentimental, you want some more 'pathetic talk.' Well, I'll have you know, I'll have you know I was laughing at you then. And I'm laughing now. Why are you trembling? Yes, laughing! I'd been insulted earlier, at dinner, by the fellows who'd come before me that evening. I went to your place to thrash one of them, the officer. But I couldn't, they were already gone; I had to vent my feelings on somebody, to get my own back, and you turned up, so I took my anger out on you and played a joke on you. I was humiliated, so I had to humiliate someone else; I was treated like a piece of trash, so I had to show my power over someone else.... That's what it was, and you thought I'd come just to save you, didn't you? You thought so, didn't you?"

I knew that she might be confused by all this, that she might fail to understand the details. But I also knew that she would understand the essence of my words very well. And so it was. She turned pale as a sheet, she wanted to say something, her lips twisted painfully. But then, as if cut down by an axe, she dropped upon a chair. And after that she listened to me with an open mouth, wide-eyed and trembling all the while with frightful shock. The cynicism, the cynicism of my words crushed her....

"Save you!" I went on, jumping up from my chair and running back and forth across the room. "Save you from what? Why, I myself may be much worse than you. Why didn't you throw it into my teeth that time, when I was lecturing you? Why didn't you say: 'And you, what did you come here for yourself? To teach me morals?' It was power, power that I needed then; I had to play with you, reduce you to tears, humble you, make you hysterical—that's what I needed! But I couldn't endure it myself, because I'm a rag, I got scared, and the devil knows what made me give you my address, like a damned fool. Well, even before I got home I was already cursing you for that address. I was already hating you because I had lied to you. Because all I could do was only play around with words, dream a bit in my mind, but in reality d'you know what I want? I want to see you all in hell, that's what! I want peace. Why, I would sell the whole world for a single kopek, just so that nobody would bother me. Should the world go to hell, or should I go without my tea now? I'll say let the world go to hell so long as I can have my tea whenever I want it. Did you know this, or didn't you?

"Well, and I know that I'm a scoundrel, scum, an egotist, a lazy good-for-nothing. I've been trembling these three days with fear that you might come. And do you know what troubled me most during these three days? That I had posed as such a hero before you, and now you'd suddenly see me in this torn old robe, penniless, vile. I told you I'm not ashamed of my poverty. Well, I'll have you know that I am ashamed, I'm more ashamed of it than of anything else, more afraid of it than of anything else, more than if I were a thief, because I'm vain, as vain as though my skin were stripped away from my body, and the very air hurts. Haven't you guessed even now that I'll never forgive you for finding me in this wretched robe, when I was flying at Apollon like a vicious pup? The awakener of conscience, the former hero, throwing himself like a mangy, shaggy mongrel upon his lackey, and the lackey laughing at him! And the tears I couldn't hold back before you, like a disgraced old woman—these too I'll never forgive you! And I'll never forgive *you* for what I'm confessing to you now! Yes, you alone will have to answer for it all, because you turned up like this, because I am myself the vilest, the most ridiculous, the pettiest, the stupidest, the most envious of all the worms on earth, who are in no way better than I am, but who—the devil knows why—never feel ashamed. And I'll get slapped by every louse all my life— that's how I am! And what do I care if you don't understand a word of all this! What do I care, what do I care about you and whether you're perishing out there or not? Why, don't you realize how much I'll hate you now, having said all this, because you were here and listened to me? Don't you know that a man will say such things only once in his lifetime, and even then when he is in hysterics! ... What do you want, then? Why are you sitting there before me after all that, why do you torture me, why don't you go?"

But suddenly a strange thing happened.

I had been so accustomed to thinking and imagining everything according to books, and picturing everything in the world as I had previously made it up in fantasy, that at the moment I didn't even grasp the meaning of this strange circumstance. And what happened was this: Liza, insulted and humiliated by me, understood much more than I had imagined. She understood out of all this what a woman, if she loves sincerely, will always understand before all else. She understood that I was myself unhappy.

The shock and hurt her face expressed gave way at first to grieved surprise. And when I began to call myself a scoundrel and scum and had burst into tears (I was in tears throughout that tirade), her whole face convulsed with a spasm. She made a move as though to get up, to stop me; and when I finished, she responded not to my shouts of "Why are you here, why don't you go!" but to the pain she knew I must have felt in telling all about myself. Besides, she was so humble, the poor thing; she considered herself infinitely beneath me; how then could she be angered or offended? She suddenly jumped up from her chair in an irrepressible impulse, and, all of her straining toward me but still timid and not daring to leave the spot, she stretched her arms to me. . . . My heart seemed to turn over. Then she rushed to me, threw her arms around my neck, and burst out crying. I broke down too and sobbed as I had never sobbed before.

"They won't let me . . . I can't be . . . good!" I said with difficulty, then stepped toward the sofa, collapsed on it face down, and for a quarter of an hour sobbed in true hysterics. She clung to me, embraced me, and remained motionless in that embrace.

Still, the trouble was that the fit of hysteria had to pass in the end. And then (I am, after all, writing the loathsome truth), lying prone on the sofa, pressing my face into the wretched leather cushion, I gradually, involuntarily, distantly at first, but irresistibly began to feel how embarrassing it would be for me now to raise my head and look straight into Liza's eyes. What was I ashamed of? I don't know, but I was ashamed. It also flashed through my overwrought mind that now our roles had been completely reversed, that she was now the heroine and I was as humbled and broken a creature as she had been that night, four days ago. . . . And all of this went through my head during the minutes when I was still lying face down on the sofa!

Good God! Could I possibly have envied her then?

I don't know. To this day I cannot decide, and at that time I was, of course, even less capable of understanding it than now. I know that I cannot live without power, without tyrannizing over someone. . . . Yet . . . yet no amount of reasoning can explain anything, and so there is no point in reasoning.

However, I mastered myself and raised my head; I'd have to raise it sometime, after all. . . . And then—I'm sure of it to this day—precisely because I was ashamed to look at her, another feeling suddenly flared up within me . . . the need to dominate and to possess. My eyes glinted with passion, and I pressed her hands hard in my own. How I hated her, and how drawn I was to her at that moment! One feeling reinforced the other. It was almost like revenge! . . . Her face at first expressed something like puzzlement, even fear, but only for a second. Then she fervently, raptly embraced me.

X

FIFTEEN MINUTES later I was running back and forth across my room in mad impatience, continually approaching the screen and peering at Liza through the crack. She sat on the floor, her head leaning against the bed; she must have been crying. But she did not leave, and this was what exasperated me. This time she knew everything. I had dealt her the final insult, yet . . . well, there is nothing more to say. She guessed that my outburst of passion was precisely my means of revenge, of inflicting new humiliation upon her, and that my previous, almost objectless hatred was now augmented by *personal, envious* hatred of her. . . . I do not insist, however, that she understood all this completely; but she realized clearly that I was a despicable man and, most important, incapable of loving her.

I know, I will be told that this is incredible—that it's impossible to be as vicious and stupid as I was; people may even add that it would be impossible not to return, or at least to appreciate, her love. But why impossible? To begin with, I was by then incapable of loving because, I repeat, to me loving meant tyrannizing and flaunting my moral superiority. I've never been able even to imagine any other kind of love, and I have now reached such a point that I sometimes think love consists precisely of the voluntary gift by the loved object of the right to tyrannize over it. Even in my underground dreams I have never conceived of love as anything but a struggle; I always began with hatred and ended with moral subjugation, after which I could not even imagine what to do with the conquered object. Besides, what is so incredible about it, when I had already managed to bring myself to such a state of moral corruption, to lose all touch with "living life" so completely, that only a few hours earlier I could reproach and shame her with the accusation that she had come to me to listen to "pathetic words." And it never occurred to me that she had come, not at all to listen to pathetic words, but to love me, for to a woman love means all of resurrection, all of salvation from any kind of ruin, all of renewal of life; indeed, it cannot manifest itself in anything but this.

Still, I did not really hate her that much when I was pacing the room and peering through the crack beyond the screen. I merely found her presence unbearable. I wanted her to disappear. I wanted "peace." I longed to remain alone in my underground. "Living life" weighed on me so heavily, unaccustomed as I was to it, that I even found it difficult to breathe.

But a few more minutes passed, and she still did not get up, as if she were unconscious. I was heartless enough to knock lightly on the screen to remind her. . . . She started suddenly, jumped up, and hurriedly began to look for her shawl, her hat and coat, as though to save herself, to escape from me. . . . Two minutes later she slowly came out from behind the screen and gave me a heavy look. I grinned viciously (however, I had to force myself to it, for *form's sake*), and turned away from her glance.

"Goodbye," she said, going to the door.

I suddenly ran up to her, seized her hand, opened it, put in . . . and closed it again. Then I immediately turned and quickly sprang away into the opposite corner, so that at least I wouldn't see....

I was about to lie just now, to write that I had done it by accident, in confusion, without thought, that I had lost my head. But I don't want to lie and therefore will say straight out that I opened her hand and slipped her...out of malice. The thought of doing this came to me while I was running back and forth across the room and she was sitting behind the screen. But this I can say with certainty: although I did this cruel thing deliberately, it was not from the heart but from my stupid head. This cruelty was so make-believe, so much a product of the mind, so purposely invented, *bookish*, that I could not endure it myself even for a moment. At first I sprang away into the corner not to see, then, in shame and desperation, I rushed out after Liza. I opened the door onto the landing and listened.

"Liza! Liza!" I called down the staircase, but timidly, quietly....

There was no answer, but it seemed to me that I heard her footfall on the steps below.

"Liza!" I cried more loudly.

No answer. But at that moment I heard the glass door leading to the street creak, opening heavily, then shutting closed again. The noise of it rose up the stairs.

She was gone. I returned to my room, bemused. I felt terribly depressed.

I stopped by the chair where she had sat and stared before me senselessly. A moment later a shock ran through my whole body; right before me on the table I saw...in short, I saw the crumpled blue five-ruble note, the note I had a moment ago closed in her hand. It was *the same* note; it could have been no other, there was no other in the house. So she had managed to throw it down when I had jumped away into the other corner.

Well? I could have expected her to do it. Could have? I

was such an egotist, I was so lacking in respect for people in reality, that I couldn't even have imagined that she might do it. I could not bear it. A moment later I rushed like a madman to dress; I quickly slipped on whatever was at hand and ran out headlong after her. She couldn't have gone two hundred steps by the time I ran out into the street.

It was quiet. The snow was tumbling down heavily, almost vertically, blanketing the sidewalk and the deserted street. There were no passersby. No sound was heard. The dreary streetlights flickered uselessly. I ran two hundred steps or so to the corner and stopped. "Where did she go, why am I running after her?"

Why? To fall down before her, to sob with repentance, to kiss her feet, to plead for forgiveness! I longed for this; my breast was torn apart, and I will never, never recall this moment without emotion. But what for? I thought. Won't I begin to hate her, even tomorrow, precisely because I kissed her feet today? Can I make her happy? Haven't I learned today again, for the hundredth time, what I am worth? Won't I torment her to death?

I stood in the snow, peering into the hazy murk and thinking about this.

"And wouldn't it, wouldn't it be better," I spoke to myself later, back at home, stifling my living heartache with phantasies, "wouldn't it be better for her now to carry away the insult with her forever? An insult! What is it but purification? It is the root of the most caustic, most painful consciousness! Why, only tomorrow I would have defiled her soul and wearied her heart. But the insult, the outrage will never die within her, and no matter how vile the filth awaiting her—the outrage will elevate and purify her... through hatred...hm...perhaps even through forgiveness.... Still, will all this make things any easier for her?"

And actually—now I am asking an idle question on my own account: which is better—cheap happiness, or noble suffering? Well, which is better?

Such were the thoughts that flitted through my mind as I sat that evening, racked, almost destroyed with the pain in my heart. Never before had I endured such anguish and remorse. Yet could there have been any doubt, when I ran out of my lodgings, that I'd turn back from halfway? I have never met Liza again, and never heard anything about her. I will also add that for a long time I remained quite pleased with the *phrase* about the beneficial effects of an insult and of hatred, though I myself had nearly fallen ill at the time with misery.

Even today, so many years later, the memory of all this is somehow too *distressing*. Many memories distress me now, but . . . shouldn't I perhaps conclude my *Notes* at this point? It seems to me that it was a mistake to start them. At any rate, I have felt ashamed throughout the writing of this narrative: hence, this is no longer literature, but corrective punishment. Because telling, for example, long tales about how I have shirked away my life through moral degeneration in my corner, through isolation from society, through loss of contact with anything alive, through vanity and malice in my underground, is really quite uninteresting. A novel requires a hero, and here there's a *deliberate* collection of all the traits for an antihero. Besides, and most importantly, all this will produce an extremely unpleasant impression, because we have all lost touch with life, we all limp, each to a greater or lesser degree.

In fact, we have lost touch so badly that we often feel a kind of loathing for genuine "living life," and hence cannot endure being reminded of it. We've reached a point where we virtually regard "living life" as hard labor, almost servitude, and we all agree in private that it's much better "according to books." And why do we sometimes fidget, why do we fuss, what are we asking for? We ourselves don't know, for, after all, it will be worse for us if our silly whims are granted. Just try, just give us, for example, more independence; untie the hands of any one of us, broaden our scope of action, relax the tutelage over us, and we... Why, I assure you, we shall immediately beg to be placed under tutelage again.

I know that you may well get angry at me for these words, you may scold and stamp your feet: "Talk about yourself and your underground miseries, but do not dare to say *'we all.'*" But if you will permit me, gentlemen, I am by no means trying to justify myself by this *we-allness*. As regards myself personally, I have in my own life merely carried to the extreme that which you have never ventured to carry even halfway; and what's more, you've regarded your cowardice as prudence, and found comfort in deceiving yourselves. So that, in fact, I may be even more "alive" than you are. Do take a closer look! Why, we don't even know where the living lives today, or what it is, or what its name is. Leave us on our own, without a book, and we shall instantly become confused and lost—we shall not know what to join, what to believe in, what to love and what to hate, what to respect and what to despise. We even feel it's too much of a burden to be men—men with real bodies, real blood *of our own*. We are ashamed of this, we deem it a disgrace, and try to be some impossible "general-humans." We are stillborn; for a long time we haven't even been begotten of living fathers, and we like this more and more. We have developed a real taste for it. We'll soon invent a way of somehow getting born from an idea. But enough; I do not want to write any more "from Underground."...

This, in truth, is not yet the end of the "Notes" of this paradoxalist. He could not keep to his resolve and went on writing. But it seems to us, too, that we may well stop here.

NOTES

1. The phrase "The lofty and the beautiful"—derived from the title of Immanuel Kant's essay "On the Lofty and the Beautiful"—was much in vogue among Russian liberal critics and intellectuals of the second quarter of the nineteenth century.

2. The phrase *"l'homme de la nature et de la vérité"* is drawn from a sentence in Jean Jacques Rousseau's *Confessions: "Je veux montrer à mes semblables un homme dans toute la vérité de la nature; et cet homme—ce sera moi."* ("I want to show to my fellow humans man in the whole truth of his nature—this man will be myself.")

3. "Descended from an ape." A reference to Charles Darwin's *The Origin of Species,* which was translated into Russian in 1864 and caused wide discussion in the Russian press. Here, as elsewhere, Dostoevsky satirizes the materialistic concept of man and his self-interest.

4. "All the Wagenheims." A reference to dentists of the period who advertised in the Petersburg newspapers.

5. "A picture of Ge." Evidently a reference to N. N. Ge, whose painting *The Lord's Supper,* exhibited at the Academy of Art in 1863, was sharply criticized by Dostoevsky as a simple, realistic genre scene, lacking depth of insight or religious feeling.

6. "As Anyone Pleases." An essay by M. Y. Saltykov-Shchedrin. The piece itself has no bearing on the

subjects discussed by Dostoevsky in *Notes from Underground*. The title was evidently seized upon merely as a pretext to snipe at Shchedrin in the course of the violent polemic between the two writers.

7. Much of Chapter VII is a polemic against the idea of "rational self-interest," advocated by the radical novelist and critic N. G. Chernyshevsky as a means of reeducating man and thus reforming society. A materialist and positivist, Chernyshevsky believed that science and reason were capable of solving all of man's problems. In his essay "The Anthropological Principle in Philosophy" (1860) he wrote: "Self-interest lies only in good deeds; and only he is rational who is good, and precisely to the extent that he is good."

8. H. T. Buckle, an English historian. His *History of Civilization in England* appeared in Russian translation in 1864–1866 and became widely popular among the progressive intelligentsia.

9. "That eternal union." A mocking allusion to the American Civil War.

10. Schleswig-Holstein, a duchy over which Austria and Prussia fought a war with Denmark in 1863–1864.

11. Stenka Razin. A Don cossack who led a bloody peasant rebellion in the seventeenth century, seizing extensive territories in southeastern Russia and along the Volga. Captured and broken on the rack as a brigand, he became a popular folk hero, whose deeds were celebrated in many songs and folktales.

12. "Crystal Palace." Another satirical reference to Chernyshevsky, in whose novel *What Is to Be Done* (1863) the grandiose "crystal palace" is described as a glorious achievement of the future communal society

(see "Vera Pavlovna's Fourth Dream"). It may also refer to the Crystal Palace built for the World Industrial Exposition in London in 1851, which represented to Dostoevsky the monstrosity of Western materialistic civilization. The description of the building in Chernyshevsky's novel coincides quite closely with the English prototype.

13. A. E. Anayevsky was a minor novelist of the time, whose works were ridiculed by critics in the 1850s and 1860s.

14. This poem (1846) by N. A. Nekrasov was widely popular among the liberal and radical intelligentsia of the time and the ensuing decades. Dostoevsky makes savage mock both of the intelligentsia and of his hero by juxtaposing the sentiment of the poem and his hero's behavior—one of many instances of the author's painful ambivalence in the *Notes from Underground*.

The choice of the epigram may also be attributed to the narrator, as yet another expression of his bitter self-mockery.

15. Preference. A gentlemen's card game.

16. Kostanzhoglo is one of the characters in the second part of Gogol's *Dead Souls*—perhaps the only positive character. A practical and just but stern landowner, he has no use for new-fangled foreign ideas but makes rational and effective use of his land and his peasants to the benefit of both himself and the peasants.

Uncle Pyotr Ivanovich is a character from I. A. Goncharov's novel *An Ordinary Story* (1847), a successful industrialist and bureaucrat, and a great believer in practical common sense and hard work.

17. "The King of Spain." A reference to the hero of Gogol's *Diary of a Madman,* a humble civil servant

who is lectured by his superior to the effect that he is "a zero, nothing more" and who ends up by going mad and imagining himself the King of Spain.

18. Lieutenant Pirogov. A character in Gogol's story "Nevsky Prospect." Pirogov's first impulse, on being thrashed by a jealous husband, is to complain to the authorities.

19. *Fatherland Notes* (*Otechestvennye Zapiski*) was an important liberal journal published from 1839 to 1884.

20. The French word *superflu* is here used in the sense of "highly refined."

21. "Manfred-like." A reference to the romantic hero of Byron's dramatic poem "Manfred" (1818)—noble, proudly solitary, tormented by a dark sin from his past, and disdainful equally of life and death.

22. Silvio is the hero of Pushkin's story "The Shot" (1830). Both the story and Lermontov's play in verse, *Masquerade* (1835), deal romantically with the theme of vengeance.

23. "And enter my home..." From Nekrasov's poem quoted in the epigraph at the beginning of Part Two.

ABOUT THE TRANSLATOR

MIRRA GINSBURG is the editor, translator, and anthologist of many important Russian authors. She has translated Yevgeny Zamyatin's *We*; four books by Mikhail Bulgakov, including *The Master and Margarita;* Andrey Platonov's *The Foundation Pit;* and several collections of Soviet science fiction. Her translation of *Notes from Underground* was dramatized at the Classic Theatre in New York in 1979. The recipient of a Guggenheim fellowship to work on the writings of Alexey Remizov, Ginsburg has also translated, adapted, and written numerous children's books.

ASK YOUR BOOKSELLER FOR
THESE BANTAM CLASSICS